Bernhard Schlink

SELF'S MURDER

Bernhard Schlink was born in Germany. He is the author of the internationally bestselling novels *The Reader* and *Homecoming*, as well as the collection of short stories *Flights of Love* and four prizewinning crime novels—*Self's Punishment* (with Walter Popp), *The Gordian Loop*, *Self's Deception*, and *Self's Murder*. He lives in Berlin and New York.

ALSO BY BERNHARD SCHLINK

Self's Punishment (with Walter Popp)
Self's Deception

The Reader
Flights of Love: Stories
Homecoming

The Gordian Loop

SELF'S MURDER

SELF'S MURDER

Bernhard Schlink

TRANSLATED FROM THE GERMAN BY
Peter Constantine

VINTAGE CRIME/BLACK LIZARD
Vintage Books
A Division of Random House, Inc.
New York

A VINTAGE CRIME/BLACK LIZARD ORIGINAL, AUGUST 2009

Grateful acknowledgment is made to Walter Popp for
his consultation on the translation.

Library of Congress Cataloging-in-Publication Data
Schlink, Bernhard.
[Selbs Mord. English]
Self's murder / Bernhard Schlink ; translated from
the German by Peter Constantine.
p. cm.
ISBN 978-0-375-70909-8
I. Constantine, Peter, 1963–   II. Title.
PT2680.L54S4513 2009
833'.914—dc22
2009002201

Book design by Christopher Zucker

www.vintagebooks.com

Printed in the United States of America
10 9 8 7 6 5 4 3 2

CONTENTS

PART ONE

PART ONE

I

In the end

In the end I did head back there.

I didn't have Nurse Beatrix sign me out. She wouldn't even let me tackle the short, easy paths leading from the Speyerer Hof Clinic to the big Ehrenfriedhof Cemetery and the Bierhelder Hof, let alone the long steep path that leads up to the Kohlhof. In vain I told her how years ago my wife and I used to go skiing on the Kohlhof: in the morning we'd head up the slope, the bus filled with people, skis, ski poles, and toboggans. Until sundown hundreds would swarm over the rutted slope, more brown than white, with its dilapidated ski jump. At lunchtime pea soup was served at the Kohlhof Restaurant. Klara had better skis than I, was a better skier, and laughed whenever I fell. I would tug at the leather straps of the bindings and grit my teeth; Amundsen had conquered the South Pole with skis that were even more antiquated. In the evening we were tired and happy.

"Let me head over to the Kohlhof, Nurse Beatrix. I'll take it easy. I want to see it again and remember old times."

"You're doing a good enough job remembering right here, Herr Self. Would you be telling me about it otherwise?"

The only thing Nurse Beatrix will allow me to do after a two-week stay at the Speyerer Hof Clinic is to walk a few steps to the elevator, ride down to the lobby, walk a few steps to the terrace, cross it, and go down some stairs to the lawn around the fountain. Nurse Beatrix is generous only when it comes to the view.

"Look at that! What a beautiful view!"

She's right. I'm sharing a room with a tax inspector who's suffering from a stomach ailment, and the view from the window is indeed panoramic and beautiful: over the trees and valleys to the Haardt Mountains. I look through the window and think how this region, where I landed by accident during the war, had grown on me and become my home. But was I to think about that all day?

So I waited until the tax inspector fell asleep after lunch, then swiftly and silently took my suit out of the closet, slipped into it, and managed to make my way to the gate without bumping into a single nurse or doctor I knew. The guard didn't care whether I was an escaping patient or a departing visitor, so I had him call me a cab.

We drove down into the valley, first between meadows and fruit trees, then through tall woods, the sun casting bright spots through the treetops onto the road and the underbrush. We drove past a wooden shack. In the old days the town had been quite a distance away, and hikers would make a last rest stop at

4

this shack before returning home. Nowadays the first houses lie off to the right after just two bends in the road, and a little farther, on the left, is the Bergfriedhof Cemetery. At the foot of the mountain we waited for the light to change, near an old kiosk that I always liked: a Greek temple, its forecourt built on a small terrace and its canopy supported by two Doric columns.

The road to Schwetzingen was open and straight, and we made quick progress. The driver told me all about his bees. From this I concluded that he must be a smoker, and asked him for a cigarette. I didn't like the taste. Then we arrived and the driver dropped me off with a promise to pick me up again in an hour to take me back.

I stood on the Schlossplatz. The building had been renovated. It was still covered in scaffolding, but the windows had been replaced and the sandstone frames of the door and window casings cleaned up. The only thing missing was a final coat of paint to make it just as spruced-up as the other buildings around the square, all three-storied and neat, with flowerboxes in the windows. There was no indication what the building would be—a restaurant, a café, a law firm, a doctor's office, a software company—and, peeking through a window, I saw only floor tarps and painters' ladders, paint cans, and rollers.

The Schlossplatz was empty except for the chestnut trees and the statue of the anonymous market wife selling asparagus. I remembered the streetcar whose rails used to end in a loop on the square. I looked over at the castle.

What did I expect? That the building's gate would open and they would all come out, stand in a row, bow, and laugh as they scattered in all directions?

A cloud covered the sun and a cold wind blew over the square. I felt a chill. Autumn hung in the air.

2

In a ditch

It all began one Sunday in February. I was heading back home to Mannheim from Beerfelden with my girlfriend, Brigitte, and her son, Manuel. Brigitte had a friend who had moved to Beerfelden from Viernheim and had invited us for a coffee-and-cake housewarming. Their children got on well together and the women talked and talked. By the time we got into the car it was already dark.

We had barely set out when it began to snow—large, heavy, wet flakes. The narrow road uphill through the woods was desolate. There was no car in front or behind, nor any coming in our direction. The snowflakes got thicker. The car swerved in the curves, the wheels skidded where the road was steep, and visibility was just enough for me to keep the car on the road. Manu, who had been chattering away, fell silent, and Brigitte kept her hands folded in her lap. Only her dog, Nonni, was asleep as if nothing was going on. The heater hadn't really kicked in, but my forehead was covered in pearls of sweat.

"Shouldn't we stop and wait for the—"

"It could snow for hours, Brigitte. And once we get snowed in, we'll be stuck."

I saw the car in the ditch only because the driver had left his headlights on, and they shone across the road like a barrier. I stopped.

"Do you want me to come with you?" Brigitte asked.

"I'll deal with it."

I got out, pulled up the collar of my jacket, and trudged through the snow. A Mercedes had strayed onto a side road and in attempting to get back onto the main road had gotten stuck in a ditch. I heard music—piano and orchestra—and through the fogged-over windows saw two men in the lighted interior, one in the driver's seat, the other diagonally behind him in the backseat. Like a steamship run aground, I thought, or an airplane after an emergency landing: the music plays on as if nothing has happened, but the journey has come to an end. I tapped on the driver's window and he lowered it a chink.

"Need help?"

Before the driver could answer the other man leaned over and opened the back door. "Thank God! Get in," he said, leaning back and motioning with his hand. Heat streamed from the interior, along with the aroma of leather and smoke. The music was so loud that the man had to raise his voice. He turned to the driver: "Turn it down, please!"

I got in. The driver took his time. He slowly reached over to the radio, fumbled for the knob, and turned it, and the music grew softer. His boss waited with a frown until it fell silent.

"We can't get out of here, and the phone isn't working. I have a feeling this is the back of beyond." He laughed bitterly, as if getting stuck were not only a mishap but some personal slight.

"Can we give you a lift?"

"Could you help push the car? If we can manage to get out of this ditch we'll be all right. There's nothing wrong with the car."

I looked at the driver, expecting him to say something. After all, he was responsible for this mess. But he didn't say anything. In the rearview mirror I could see his eyes fixed on me.

The boss saw my questioning look. "Why don't I get in the driver's seat, and you and Gregor push? What we need . . ."

"No." The driver turned around. A mature face and a low, hoarse voice. "I'll stay here, and you do the pushing." I heard an accent, but I couldn't quite place it.

The boss was the younger of the two, but looking at his delicate hands and slender build, I couldn't make rhyme or reason of the driver's suggestion. However, the boss did not contradict him. We got out. The driver stepped on the gas and we pushed against the car, the spinning wheels whirring and flinging out snow, pine needles, leaves, and mud. We went on pushing, it went on snowing, and our hair got wet, our hands and ears numb. Brigitte and Manu came over. I had them sit on the car's trunk, and when I got on it, too, the wheels made contact and the car lurched out of the ditch with a jolt.

"Get home safely!" I called out after them, and we headed back to our car.

"Wait a minute!" The boss came running after us. "Who should I thank for rescuing us?"

I found a card in my jacket pocket and handed it to him. "'Gerhard Self.'"

He blew the flakes off the card and read aloud: "'Private investigator.' You are . . . You are a detective? Then I have a job for you. Can you drop by my office?" He rummaged around in his pockets for a card but didn't find one. "My name is Welker, and it's the bank at the Schlossplatz in Schwetzingen. Will you remember that?"

3

A job's a job

I didn't go to Schwetzingen the following day, nor the day
after. In fact, I had no intention of going. Our encounter that
stormy night on the Hirschhorner Höhe, and his invitation,
reminded me of the promises one makes with holiday
acquaintances. They never work out.

But a job's a job, and a case is a case. I had spent last fall
investigating the sick-leave claims of salesladies at the Tengel-
mann department store chain, and had managed to catch one
or two who were feigning illness. That was about as reward-
ing as being a train conductor on the lookout for fare
dodgers. In the winter no cases came my way. It's just the way
of the world: one doesn't hire a private detective who is over

seventy as a bodyguard, or send him around the world to chase down stolen jewels. Even a department store chain that wants to spy on its sales staff will be more impressed by a younger fellow with a cell phone and a BMW who's a former cop turned private investigator than by an old guy driving an old Opel.

Not that I didn't manage to keep myself busy all winter without cases. I cleaned my office at the Augustaanlage, waxed and polished the wooden floors, and washed the window. It is a big window; the office used to be a tobacconist's store, and the window was for display. I cleaned my apartment, around the corner in the Richard-Wagner-Strasse, and put my cat, Turbo, who's getting too fat, on a diet. I showed Manu *The Execution of Emperor Maximilian of Mexico* in the Kunst halle museum, and the Suebenheim burial mounds at the Reiss Museum. In the Landesmuseum für Technik und Arbeit I showed him the electrified chairs and beds that were used in the nineteenth century in attempts to drive tapeworms out of people's intestines. I took Manu to the Sultan Selim mosque and to the synagogue. On TV we watched Bill Clinton being sworn into office. In the Luisenpark we went to see the storks, which had not flown to Africa this winter, and walked all the way down the bank of the Rhine to the Strandbad—its closed restaurant white, unapproachable, and dignified, like an English seaside casino in winter. I tried to convince myself that I was relishing the opportunity to do everything I'd always wanted to but couldn't find time for.

Until Brigitte asked me: "Why are you always going shopping? And why don't you go during the day, when the stores are empty, instead of in the evening, when they're packed? That's the kind of thing old people do." Her questions went on. "And is that why you eat lunch at the Nordsee and the Kaufhof? When you had time on your hands, you always used to do your own cooking."

A few days before Christmas I couldn't make it up the stairs to my apartment. I felt as if my chest were clamped in iron, my left arm hurt, and my head was, in a strange way, both clear and befuddled. I sat down on the first landing until Herr and Frau Weiland came and helped me up to the top floor, where our apartments are across from each other. I lay down on my bed and fell asleep, slept through the whole of the following day, the day after that, and Christmas Eve. When Brigitte came looking for me on Christmas Day, first irritated and then worried, I did get up, and had some of her roast beef along with a glass of red wine. But for weeks afterward I was tired and could not exert myself without breaking out in a sweat and getting out of breath.

"You had a heart attack, Gerhard, and not a small one at that—I'd say a medium one. You should've been in intensive care," said my friend Philipp, a surgeon at the Mannheim municipal hospital, shaking his head when I told him later about it. "There's no messing with the old ticker. If you aggravate it you'll end up biting the dust."

He sent me to his internist colleague, who wanted to push a tube from my groin into my heart. A tube from my groin into my heart! I told him thanks, but no thanks.

4

Silent partner

The lady I do all my banking with at the Badische Beamten-bank knew the name Welker, and the bank on the Schlossplatz in Schwetzingen. "Weller and Welker. It's the oldest private bank in the whole Palatinate area. Back in the seventies and eighties it was struggling to survive, but it's pulled through. I hope you aren't thinking of leaving us."

I called and was put through to Welker's office. "Ah, Herr Self. I'm so glad you called. Today or tomorrow's fine, though I'd much rather . . ." His words became muffled for a few seconds as he covered the mouthpiece. Then: "Could you come over today at two?"

The road was dry. The snow at the sides had turned grimy.

It had dripped from the trees and dried in the furrows of the fields. Beneath a gray, low-hanging sky the traffic signs, guardrails, houses, and fences were waiting for spring, and a spring cleaning.

The bank Weller & Welker was marked only by a small tarnished brass plate. I rang the bell and a door within a large gate swung open. The entry was vaulted and paved. Three steps on the left led to another door, which opened as the first one closed. I climbed the stairs and felt as if I had stepped into another era. The bank counters were carved of dark wood and had wooden bars. The panels next to them were inlaid with blond wood: a cogwheel, two crossed hammers, a wheel with wings, a mortar and pestle, and the barrel of a cannon. The bench at the far end of the room was of the same dark wood and had dark green velvet cushions. The walls were covered in shimmering dark green fabric, and the ornate ceiling was also of dark wood.

The room was silent. There was no rustle of bills, no clinking of coins, no hushed voices. I didn't see behind the lattice any men with mustaches, hair plastered on scalps, pencils behind ears, leather sleeve patches, or rubber-banded upper arms, which would have been appropriate here, nor did I see their modern counterparts. I stepped closer to the counter, saw the dust on the bars of the lattice, and was about to peer through when suddenly the door across from the entrance opened.

The driver was standing in the doorway. "Herr Self, I—"

He didn't manage to finish the sentence. Welker came rushing past him toward me. "I'm so glad you were able to come. My last client's just left. Let's go upstairs."

Behind the door there was a steep narrow staircase. I followed Welker up and the driver followed me. The stairs opened into a large office with partitions, desks, computers, phones, a number of young men sporting dark suits and serious faces, and an occasional young woman or two. Welker and the driver swiftly escorted me through to the executive office, which had a view of the Schlossplatz. I was ushered to a leather sofa while Welker settled into one chair and the driver the other.

Welker waved his hand with a broad welcoming gesture. "Gregor Samarin is one of the family. You see, he likes to drive, and he's better at it than I am . . ." Welker saw my surprise. "No, he does like driving and is good at it, which is why he was at the wheel the other day when we met. But that's not his job. His job is to see to all practical matters." Welker looked over at Samarin as if to check whether he agreed.

Samarin nodded slowly. He must have been in his early fifties. He had a large head, a receding hairline, and protruding light blue eyes. His colorless hair was cut short. He sat confidently, with his legs apart.

Welker didn't continue right away. At first I thought he might be weighing what he wanted to say, but then I wondered if there wasn't a message in his silence. But what message? Or did he want to give me an opportunity to take everything in: the atmosphere, Gregor Samarin, himself? He had been particularly attentive and polite when he greeted me and walked me to his office. I could see him as a suave host, or at a diplomatic or academic affair. Was his silence a question of style, old-school good breeding? He struck me as a man of breeding: clear, sensitive, intelligent features; good posture; measured movements. At the same time he struck me as sad, and though a certain cheerfulness flitted over his face when he greeted me or smiled, a shadow would quickly darken it once more. It was not just a shadow of sadness. I noticed something sullen and sulking about his mouth, a disappointment, as if fate had cheated him out of some promised indulgence.

"We're about to celebrate our two-hundredth anniversary, a major event for which my father wants a history of our establishment. I've been working on it for some time, whenever I can get away from business, and as grandfather had done some research and left some notes, my task isn't difficult, except in one matter."

He hesitated, brushed a few strands of hair from his forehead, leaned back, and glanced at Samarin, who was sitting motionless. "In 1873, the stock exchanges in both Vienna and Berlin collapsed. The depression lasted until 1880—long enough for the days of the private banker to become numbered. The era of the big stock banks and savings banks had begun, and some private bankers who survived the depression turned their enterprises into joint stock corporations. Others merged; others simply gave up. Our bank prevailed."

Again he hesitated. I no longer get irritated; in earlier days I would have. I hate it when people beat about the bush.

"Our bank prevailed not only because my great-grandfather and great-great-grandfather were good businessmen, and the old Wellers, were, too. Since the 1870s, we had had a silent partner, who by the time of the First World War had brought in around half a million. That might not sound like a lot to you, but let me tell you, it was a significant amount. The long and short of it is that I can't write a history of our bank without also focusing on this silent partner. However"—this time he paused for dramatic effect—"I don't know who this partner was. My father doesn't know the partner's name, my grandfather doesn't mention him in his notes, and I haven't found it in any of the documents."

"A very silent partner indeed."

He laughed, and for a moment had a youthful, rascally look about him. "I'd be grateful if you could make him speak."

"You want me to—"

"I'd like you to find out who this silent partner was. His name, his birth and death dates, what he did for a living, who his family was. Did he have children? Is one of his great-grandsons going to come knocking at my door, asking for his share?"

"Wasn't this silent partnership terminated?"

He shook his head. "After 1918, my grandfather's notes don't mention anything about it anymore. No mention of the partnership, nor of any more money being brought in, nor anything about settling accounts or buying anyone out. Somehow the partnership came to an end. Now I can't really imagine any great-grandsons suddenly turning up. Anyone who had a large pile of money stashed away with us would have had ample reason in all these years to come claim it."

"Why don't you hire a historian? I bet there are hundreds of them who get degrees every year and can't find a job—they'd jump at the chance to go looking for lost partners."

"I've tried my luck with history students and retired professors. It was a disaster. I ended up knowing less than when I started. No"—he shook his head—"I've chosen you for a reason. One could argue that your job and theirs is the same: historians and detectives both go after truths that are buried and forgotten, and yet the methods are quite different. Maybe your approach will get better results than those history fellows.' Take a few days, cast about a bit, follow different leads. If nothing comes up, then nothing comes up—I'll get over it." He picked up a checkbook and a fountain pen from the table and placed them on his knees. "How much should I give you as an advance?"

I'd do some casting about for a few days—if he wanted to pay me for that, then why not?

"Two thousand. My fee's a hundred an hour, plus expenses. I'll provide you with a detailed breakdown once I'm done."

He wrote out the check, handed it to me, and got up. "I hope you'll get back to me soon. I'll be here at the office, so if you prefer dropping by to calling, I'd be delighted."

Samarin walked me down the stairs and past the tellers. When we reached the door he took me by the arm. "Herr Welker's wife died last year, and he's been working day and night ever since. He shouldn't have taken on the history of the bank on top of everything else. I'd be grateful if you would call me should you come up with something or if you need anything. I want to lighten his load any way I can." Samarin peered at me expectantly.

"How do the names Welker, Weller, and Samarin go together?"

"What you mean is, how does Samarin fit in with Weller and Welker. It doesn't. My mother was Russian and worked as an interpreter during the war. She died when she gave birth to me. The Welkers were my foster parents."

He was still peering at me expectantly. Was he waiting for confirmation that I'd come to him and not to Welker?

I said good-bye. The door didn't have a handle, but next to it was a button. I pressed it and the door opened, then fell shut behind me with a loud snap. I gazed over the empty square and was pleased with the job and the check in my pocket.

5

The Gotthard Tunnel and
the Andes Railway

At the University of Mannheim library I located a history of German banking: three fat volumes filled with text, numbers, and graphs. I managed to check them out and take them with me. Back at my office I sat down and began to read. The traffic hummed outside, then came twilight and darkness. The Turk from next door, who sells newspapers, cigarettes, and bric-a-brac of every kind, closed his shop, and when he saw me by the lamp at my desk he knocked at the door and wished me a pleasant evening. I didn't go home until my eyes began to hurt, and was once again poring over the books when the Turk opened his shop in the morning and the children who were always his first customers were buying their chewing gum and Gummi Bears. By afternoon I had finished.

I've never had much interest in banking—and why should I? Whatever I earn ends up in my checking account, and what I need on a daily basis gets drawn from there, as do payments for health insurance, social security, and life insurance. There are times when more money accumulates in my account than gets withdrawn, and what I do then is buy a few shares of Rhineland Chemical Works stock and put the certificates in my safe. They lie there untouched as the market rises and falls.

And yet banking and its history is anything but dull. In those three volumes I found quite a few references to the Weller & Welker Bank. It was founded toward the end of the eighteenth century when Herr Weller, a Swabian who was a sales and freight expeditor in Stuttgart, and Herr Welker from Baden, who had been banker to one of the prince elector's cousins, formed a partnership. They began with currency transactions and bills of exchange but soon moved on to government loans and securities. Their bank was too small to assume a leading role in any important ventures, but it was such a reliable and reputable establishment that larger banks were happy to involve them in projects, such as the founding of the Rhineland Chemical Works, the launching of the Mannheim Municipal Loan in 1868 that funded the construction of the Mannheim-Karlsruhe railroad, and the financing of the Gotthard Tunnel. Weller & Welker had a particularly lucky hand in Latin American ventures, ranging from Brazilian and Colombian government loans to involvement in the Vera Cruz and Mexico railroad and the Andes line.

Theirs is a history that can hold its own alongside that of

other private banks that not only have a history but have made history: the Bethmanns, Oppenheims, and Rothschilds. The author regretted that he was not able to write more about private banks; they kept their archives under lock and key, and if they did open them it was only to scholars they commissioned to do research for jubilees and commemorative tributes. Private banks gave their archival records to public archives only in cases of liquidation, or of foundations being established.

I took out a pack of Sweet Aftons from the filing cabinet where I lock up my cigarettes so that when I want a smoke I don't just open a pack but have to get up, go over to the filing cabinet, and unlock it. Brigitte hopes this will make me smoke less. I lit a cigarette. Welker had mentioned only his own documents, not the bank's archives. Had the bank Weller & Welker dissolved its archives and disposed of their contents? I put a call through to the state archives in Karlsruhe, and the official responsible for industry and banking was still in the office. No, the archives of Weller & Welker were not on deposit with them. No, they were not on deposit at any other public archive, either. No, he could not say with certainty if the bank had an archive. Private archives are only randomly collected and preserved. But hell would freeze over before a private bank would—

"And we're not talking about any old bank," I cut in. "Weller and Welker was founded almost two centuries ago. The bank cofinanced the Gotthard Tunnel and the Andes Railroad." I was boasting a little with my newly acquired knowledge. And they say boasting gets you nowhere.

"Ah, *that* bank! Didn't they also finance the Michelstadt-Eberbach Railroad? Could you hold on for a second?"

I heard him put down the receiver, push back a chair, and open and shut a drawer. "In Schwetzingen there's a certain Herr Schuler who is involved with the archives of that bank. He's researching the history of the Baden railways and kept us quite busy with his questions."

"Do you happen to have Schuler's address?"

"Not at hand. It must be in the file with our correspondence. I'm not certain, though, if I can . . . I mean, it's personal information, isn't it? And it would be confidential, wouldn't it? May I ask why you want his address?"

But I had already taken out the white pages, opened them to Schwetzingen, and found the teacher Adolf Schuler, retired. I thanked the official and hung up.

6

No fool

The retired teacher Adolf Schuler lived behind the palace gardens in a tiny house that wasn't much bigger than the nearby garden sheds. I looked in vain for a bell and knocked on the door, then walked through the slushy snow of the garden to the back of the house, where I found the kitchen door open. He was sitting by the stove, eating out of a pot while reading a book. Heaped on the table, the floor, the refrigerator, the washing machine, the sideboard, and the cupboards were books, files, dirty dishes, empty and full cans and bottles, moldy bread, rotting fruit, and dirty laundry. There was a sour, musty smell in the air. Schuler himself stank. His breath reeked and his spattered tracksuit gave off a haze of old sweat. He wore a sweat-rimmed cap the way Americans do, and wire-rimmed spectacles on his nose, and so many age spots covered his wrinkled face that his skin had acquired a dark complexion.

He did not protest at my suddenly appearing in his kitchen. I introduced myself as a retired official from Mannheim who now has all the time in the world to occupy himself with the history of railroads, for which he's always had a passion. At first Schuler was grumpy, but he warmed up when he saw my pleasure at the wealth of knowledge he displayed. He led me through the burrows of his house, which was chock-full of books and papers, from one cavern to the next, from one hallway to the next, picking up a book here, pulling out a file there to show me. After a while he did not seem to notice or care that I was no longer asking questions about the involvement of Weller & Welker in the building of the Baden railways.

He told me about Estefania Cardozo, a Brazilian woman who had been a lady-in-waiting at the court of Pedro II, whom old Herr Weller had married in 1834 during a journey through Central and South America. They had a son who as a youth had absconded to Brazil and set up a business there, and returned to Schwetzingen with his Brazilian wife after the death of old Herr Weller. There he ran the bank with young Welker. Schuler told me of the centenary celebration in the palace gardens, which had been attended by the grand duke. There a lieutenant from Baden, one of the Welker clan, and a lieutenant from the grand duke's entourage got into an argument. This resulted in a duel the following morning, at which, to Schuler's great pride as a man from Baden, the Prussian lieutenant fell. He also told me of a sixteen-year-old Welker who in the summer of 1914 had fallen in love with Weller's fifteen-year-old daughter, and because he could not get permission to marry her enlisted right at the outbreak of the war, seeking and finding death in the bravura of a foolish cavalry charge.

"At sixteen?"

"What is sixteen too young for? For death? For war? For love? The Weller girl had inherited Portuguese and Indian blood from her mother and grandmother, so by fifteen she was already a woman who could turn men's heads and make their senses reel."

He took me to a wall covered with photographs and showed me a young woman with large dark eyes, full lips, a rich cascade of curls, and a pained, haughty expression. She was spectacularly beautiful, and had still been so as an old woman, as the picture hanging next to the first one testified.

"But their parents considered them too young for marriage," I said.

"It wasn't a question of age. Both families had agreed not to allow their children to marry. They did not want the two partners to end up as brothers-in-law or cousins, adding family quarrels to potential business conflicts. Well, the children could have eloped and faced being disinherited, but they weren't strong enough. With the last Welker, though, it wasn't a problem anymore. Bertram was an only child, as was Stephanie, and their parents were happy enough that the money would remain in the family. There's not much left anymore."

"She died?"

"She fell to her death last year when the two of them were on a mountain hike. Her body was never found." Schuler was silent, and I didn't say anything, either. He knew what I was thinking. "There was a police investigation," he continued. "There always is in such cases, but he was cleared. They had spent the night in a hut. He was still asleep in the morning when she went out onto a glacier that he hadn't wanted to hike on. Didn't you read about it? It was all over the papers."

"Did they have any kids?"

He nodded. "Two—a boy and a girl. They're now at a boarding school in Switzerland."

I nodded, too. Yes, yes, life's tough. He sighed, and I made a few commiserating sounds. He shuffled into the kitchen, took a can of beer out of the refrigerator, picked up a dirty glass from the table, wiped at it with the sleeve of his track-suit, struggled to open the can with his gouty fingers, and poured half the contents into the glass. With his left hand he held out the glass to me, but I took the can out of his right hand and said, "Cheers!"

"Here's to you!"

We drank.

"Are you the archivist of Weller and Welker?"

"What makes you say that?"

"The official at the state archives talks of you as if you are colleagues."

"Well . . ." He burped. "I wouldn't say I was a colleague, exactly, nor could you call this a real archive. Old Herr Welker was interested in the history of his bank and asked me to put all the old files in order. We knew each other from school, old Herr Welker and I, and were like friends. He sold me this house for next to nothing, and I tutored his son and his grandchildren, and whenever we could help each other out we did so. His cellar was full of old things, as was his attic. No one had the slightest idea what was there or knew where anything was. Nobody ended up doing anything with it."

"What about you?"

"What about me? When Old Herr Welker had the storage area renovated, he had lights, ventilation, and heating installed in the cellar. So here are all the old things, and I'm still busy sorting it all out. Well—perhaps you *could* say that I'm the bank's archivist."

"And every year you acquire more old files. It sounds like a Sisyphean task."

"That it is." He headed back to the refrigerator, took out two beers, and gave me one. Then he looked me in the eye. "I used to be a teacher, and all my life had to listen to my pupils' clever or silly lies, their excuses, their explanations, their little dodges. This place is a mess. My niece keeps telling me that, and I know it myself. I can't smell a thing: no good smells, no bad smells, no flowers, no perfumes. I can't tell if the food is burning on the stove or the clothes on the ironing board. I can't even tell if I stink. And yet"—he took the cap off his head and ran his fingers over his bald pate—"I'm no fool. Are you going to tell me who you really are and what it is you really want?"

7

C, L, or Z

Once a teacher always a teacher, and for a good teacher we all remain pupils, no matter how old we might be. I told him who I was and what I was looking for. Perhaps I did this because of our age; the older I get, the readier I am to assume that people as old as I am will be on my side. And I did want to know what he might have to say.

"The silent partner . . . That's an old story. Bertram's right," he told me. "His silent share was about half a million, about as large as that of both families, and stopped the bank from having to declare bankruptcy. We don't know his name, and the Welkers and Wellers I've known in my time and who are now dead didn't know, either. I'm not saying we knew nothing about him. He sent letters from Strasbourg and so must have lived there. He was in the legal profession, perhaps a company attorney or a lawyer, or maybe even a professor. When the syndicates came up in the 1880s Weller and Welker took an interest in them, and he clarified for them how to set one up legally, and what the legal aspects would be. In 1887, he thought about moving to Heidelberg; there's a letter in which he seeks information concerning a house or apartment. But in lieu of a legible signature, we have only an initial—a C, L, or Z—and it's unclear whether it stood for a first name or a surname, because though he seemed to be on the friendliest terms with both Weller and Welker, in those days one could be the best of friends with someone and still address him by his surname."

"There can't have been that many men in the legal profession in Strasbourg. A hundred? Two hundred? What do you think?" I cut in.

"Let's say there were six hundred in all during the period in question. With those initials I'd say there'd be at most a hundred, half of whom can be eliminated since they did not live there the entire time. To follow up on the remaining fifty would be a lot of work, but it's doable. Old Herr Welker didn't think it was worth pursuing, which was my view, too. As for Bertram not being able to write the history of the bank without the silent partner's name, that's nonsense. One thing I'd like to know is why he didn't come to me with his request, but to you?" Schuler was working himself into a rage. "In fact, why doesn't anyone ever come to me? I sit in my cellar and nobody comes to me. Am I a mole, a rat, a wood louse?"

"You're a badger. Look at your burrow: caves, tunnels, entries and exits buried in a mountain of files."

"A badger!" He slapped his thighs. "A badger! Follow me; I'll show you my other burrow."

He hurried out into the garden, waving dismissively when I pointed out that he had left the kitchen door ajar. He pulled the garden gate open and started his car. It was a BMW-Isetta, a model from the 1950s in which the front wheels are farther apart than the back wheels, and the front of the car is also the door, which claps open with the steering wheel—the kind of vehicle for which you need a driver's license not for a car, but for a motorbike. I sat down next to him and we went chugging off.

The old warehouse was not far from the Schlossplatz. It was an elongated three-story building with offices and apartments whose former function was no longer evident. In the eighteenth century the Wellers, when they were still sales and freight expeditors, had had their Palatine center here, with a countinghouse, stables, lofts, and a two-level cellar. Schuler had stored the boxes with the unexamined material in the lower cellar, while in the upper cellar the material he had already been through lined the shelves on the walls. There was again that sour, musty smell. At the same time the aroma of the glue Schuler used for his scrapbooks hung pleasantly in the air. There was bright daylight in the upper cellar. The lawn outside was so low-lying that there was space for a large window. This was where Schuler worked, and he had me sit at the table. I saw the abundance of files as an irredeemable jumble, but Schuler knew exactly what was where, reached for everything with ease, untied one bundle of files after another, and spread out his finds before me.

"Herr Schuler!"

"Here, for instance, we have—"

"Herr Schuler!"

He put the files down.

"You don't have to prove to me that what you said was true. I believe you."

"Then why doesn't *he* believe me? Why didn't he tell *me* anything, why didn't he ask *me*?" Schuler was again talking himself into a rage, waving his hands and arms about and sending out waves of the odor of sweat.

I tried to calm him down. "The bank is going through a crisis. Welker's lost his wife and has had to send his children away—you can't expect him to be thinking files and archives. He only sent me looking for the silent partner because he happened to meet me."

"You really think so?" He sounded doubting and hopeful.

I nodded. "I bet all of this is very difficult for him. He doesn't strike me as particularly hardy."

Schuler thought it over. "It's true—late children are the delicate ones, and because they come along late in life they get fussed over all the more. When Bertram was born in 1958, his parents were over forty. He was a sweet boy, talented, somewhat dreamy, and quite spoiled. A child of Germany's boom years, if you know what I mean. But you're right: it can't be easy for him without Stephanie and the children—and it was only a few years back that his parents died in a car crash." He shook his head. "Here you have a man who had everything you could wish for in life, and then . . ."

8

Women!

That evening I cooked some polenta with pork medallions and an olive-anchovy sauce for Brigitte and Manu. We sat at the large table in my kitchen.

"A man has a wife and two children, and together with his wife a whole lot of money. One day husband and wife go hiking in the mountains. He comes back alone."

"He killed her," Manu said, flicking his index finger across his neck. He's always been outspoken, and even more so since his voice broke. This worries Brigitte and, single mother that she is, she expects me to stand by her and be a sensitive and steadfast male role model for her son.

She eyed us severely. "Perhaps it was a tragic accident. Why are you both always jumping to—"

"How come you didn't cook spaghetti?" Manu cut in. "I don't like this yellow stuff."

"It might well have been an accident. But let's suppose that he did in fact murder her. Would it have been for the money?"

"Might he have had a paramour?" Manu proposed.

"What?" We had underestimated the range of Manu's vocabulary.

"Well, a woman he was screwing."

"Nowadays one doesn't have to murder one's wife because of a paramour. You can divorce your wife and marry the paramour," Brigitte said.

"But then there goes half the money. Gerhard just told us that they had a lot of money together. And why marry a paramour?"

"I really like the polenta," Brigitte said, "and the meat and the sauce, too—and you cooked for us and got the merlot I like. You're such a sweetheart." She raised her glass. "But you men are fools. He came back alone, you said?"

I nodded. "That's right. And her body was never found."

"There you go!" Brigitte said. "She's not dead. She had a lover and went off with him. And as for the husband who never cared for her, serves him right."

"Nice try, Mom," Manu chimed in. "But it doesn't pan out. If everyone thinks she's dead, how does she get at the money?"

It was my turn. "That's the last thing on her mind. Even if her lover is only a golf or tennis pro, he's the love of her life, and love is worth more than all the money in the world."

Brigitte looked at me pityingly, as if among foolish men I were a particular fool. "It wasn't just the money the husband and the wife had together; they also ran the business together. And the wife—I'm sorry to have to put it this way—happens to be the cleverer: she siphons off money behind his back and opens an account in Costa Rica. That's where she's living with her lover, a young painter. And because she can't sit still, she's back in business and has made a fortune supplying the Costa Rican market with chocolate marshmallows."

"Why Costa Rica?"

"Astrid and Dirk went there and loved it. Why don't we ever go to such places on vacation? Both Manu and I speak Portuguese, and the only thing down there that got on Astrid's and Dirk's nerves was that they had to speak English and everyone took them for gringos."

"Mom?"

"Yes, Manu?"

"What about the children? If the wife goes to Costa Rica with her lover, does she just forget her children?"

Manu had been raised for many years by his father in Brazil. Brigitte has never discussed with him why she allowed his father to take him there, nor has Manu brought up how he felt about it, then or now. He peered at her with his dark eyes.

She peered back at him, and then at her plate. When her tears dropped onto the polenta she said, "Oh, damn!" and picked up the napkin from her lap, put it beside her plate, pushed her chair back, got up, and left the room. Manu's eyes followed her. After a few moments he got up, too, and went to the door. He looked back at me, shrugged his shoulders, and grinned. "Women!"

Later, when Manu and Turbo had fallen asleep in front of

the TV, we tucked Manu in and went off to bed, where we lay next to each other, lost in thought. Why had Welker hired me? Because he had murdered his wife on account of the money, and was now worried that a descendant of the silent partner might demand his share? Was he more worried about this than he had admitted? But why hadn't he sent Schuler in search of the silent partner? For that matter, why hadn't he sent me to Schuler? I could not imagine that Schuler and the archive had just slipped his mind, nor could I imagine that all this had to do with his writing the history of the bank. But it didn't really make sense, either, that he'd have killed his wife. Does one murder one's wife and then hire a private investigator, someone who's notoriously inquisitive and wary, a regular snoop? Then I thought about the conversation we'd had at dinner and laughed.

"Why are you laughing?"

"You're a wonderful woman."

"Are you about to propose?"

"An old fool like me?"

"Come here, you old fool."

She turned toward me and in her arms I felt as if I were being washed over by big waves, then soft ones, and then a calm sea.

I felt her tears as she nestled up to me to go to sleep.

"Things will work out just fine with Manu," I whispered. "You'll see."

"I know," she whispered back. "And you? Your case?"

I decided not to go to my old friend, Chief Inspector Nägelsbach, nor to look into Frau Welker's death, nor to go looking for the father Welker had mentioned—and who, since Welker's father was dead, would have to be old Herr

Weller. I decided not to look into how the bank had recovered financially and what its current situation was. I would leave all that and, following the correct procedure for a fair-and-square private investigator, inform my client of the progress of my investigation and ask if he wanted me to follow the Strasbourg lead.

"My case? I think I can handle it."

But she was already asleep.

9

An ongoing process

At first the fact that I couldn't reach Welker didn't get on my nerves. I was invariably told, pleasantly enough, that he was in conference. Would I not like to speak to Herr Samarin instead? The following morning the friendly woman's voice informed me that Herr Welker would be out of the office all day, but that I was welcome to try him again tomorrow—though she could put me through to Herr Samarin, if I liked. She renewed the offer the following day, and informed me regretfully that Herr Welker was still out of the office and wouldn't be back till later.

"When?"

"I couldn't say. But Herr Samarin might know. One moment, please."

"Hello, Herr Self? How's your investigation coming along?"

Though his accent came across stronger on the phone, I still could not place it.

"It's coming along fine. When's your boss due back?"

"We were expecting him yesterday and think he'll be in today. Not that I can guarantee it; he might not be in till tomorrow. I suggest you call back next week. Unless I can be of service?"

Later I got a call from Schuler, who was irate and fuming. "What did you tell Bertram Welker about me?"

"Not a word. I didn't even get to—"

"Then may I ask why Gregor Samarin, his damn lackey, wouldn't let me see him? I was Gregor's teacher, too, and he was my pupil, even if quite a stubborn one. How dare he tell me in that tone that he knows everything and that he doesn't need me, and Bertram doesn't need me, either?"

"Herr Welker has been out of the office for the past few days. Why—"

"Balderdash! I saw Bertram and Gregor pulling up in their car when I got there. I don't know if Bertram recognized me. I don't think he did, otherwise he'd never have left me standing there."

"When was this?"

"Just now."

I put another call through to the bank, but was again told that Herr Welker was away. Now my curiosity was piqued, and I drove over to Schwetzingen. The sun was shining, the snow was gone, and little snowdrops were blossoming in the gardens. Spring was in the air. On the Schlossplatz in Schwetzingen the first strollers were out and about; young men casually draped their sweaters over their shoulders, and the girls' short blouses revealed their navels. The cafés had put out a few tables where people with warm coats could sit.

I sat outside until the sun disappeared and it grew colder. I smoked and drank tea, Earl Grey, which goes well with my Sweet Afton cigarettes. I could see everyone who entered or left the bank, and all the bustling about in the large office area on the second floor: the back-and-forth, people getting up and sitting down. In Welker's office the metallic chain curtains were drawn shut, revealing nothing. But as I got up to go inside the café to sit by the window, the curtains parted and Welker opened the window, leaned on the sill, and looked out over the square. I darted into the café, from where I could see him gazing into the distance. He shook his head, and after a while closed the window. The curtain was drawn shut again and the lights went on.

There weren't many pedestrians in the streets. The bank's few customers mostly pulled up in their cars; they drove up to the gate, which swung open to let them in, and about half an hour later let them out again. At five o'clock, four young women left the bank, and at seven, three young men. In Welker's office the lights remained on till nine thirty. I worried that I might not make it to my car fast enough to be able to tail him. But I stood on the square waiting in vain for the gate to swing open and for him to drive out or to emerge from the door within the gate. The bank lay in darkness. After a while I sauntered across the square and around the block. I didn't find another entrance to the bank, but from a neighboring yard that was accessible from the street I got a rear view of the bank's roof. It had been built out, and the windows and balcony door were brightly lit. I could make out paintings on some of the walls, and I could tell that the curtains were made of fabric. These weren't more offices; this was an apartment.

I didn't head back home right away. I called Babs, an old girlfriend, a German-and French-language teacher. She never went to bed before midnight.

"Sure, come by," she said.

She was grading papers, sitting over a second bottle of red wine and a full ashtray. I told her all about my case and asked her to contact a detective agency in Strasbourg for me and have them look into lawyers bearing the initials C, L, or Z who had lived in Strasbourg between 1885 and 1918. I don't know any French.

"What's the name of the detective agency?"

"I'll let you know tomorrow morning. I once worked with them on a case back in the early fifties. I hope they're still there."

"How did you manage to get by without knowing French?"

"The guy I was working with knew German. But he was already of a certain age, so he can't possibly still be with us. A young man from Baden-Baden had gotten involved with the Foreign Legion—he'd been abducted, by all accounts—and we managed to find out his whereabouts. It wasn't us, though, who got him out. Heaven and earth had to be set in motion, ambassadors and bishops. We did, however, give thought to how we might give it a try. Can you imagine a German-French commando going out on a mission just a few years after the war?"

She laughed. "You miss the old times? When you were young and strong and on a roll?"

"On a roll? Even during the war I wasn't on a roll, let alone afterward. Or do you mean I'm preoccupied with growing old? In the past I used to think that one day one starts aging, and that a few years later one's done and is old. But it's nothing like that. Aging's an ongoing process; you're never done."

"I'm looking forward to my pension. I don't like teaching anymore. The kids do their thing. They plod through school, and then through job training, and don't let anything get to them: no book, no idea, no feelings of love. I no longer like them."

"What about your own kids?"

"Them I love. You can't believe how pleased I was when Röschen finally let her hair grow out and stopped coloring it green. You know she finished high school with honors and got a grant from the German National Academic Foundation? And after only two semesters of business administration she spent a year at the London School of Economics. Even as a student she's already earning more than I am as a veteran teacher."

I shook my head in disbelief.

"She's set up a small and successful fund-raising firm. She's built up and is expanding a mammoth database with the help of some students whom she pays minimum wage, because in fund-raising everything depends on whose birthday falls on what day, when a company is celebrating its anniversary, the personal interests of possible donors, and what kinds of lives their ancestors lived. The other day she said to me, 'Mom, do you think it's a good idea for me to rope in some Eastern

opean students who're studying German? I could cut my
or costs in half.'"

"So what did you tell her?"

"'Good idea,' I said, and told her she might want to set up
those students with computers instead of paying them wages,
and let them pay off the computers with their work for her.
Needless to say, old computers that are being phased out
here—over in Eastern Europe they've no need for modern
computers."

"So?"

"She thought my suggestion was great. But come to think
of it, why don't you send my eldest to Strasbourg? It's not
really a detective job—it's more like historical research—and
now that he's spent three semesters in Dijon, his French is better than mine. He passed his exams but has time on his hands,
as he's not starting his job at the industrial tribunal till May."

"Does he still live in Jungbusch?"

"Yes. Give him a call."

10

So funny you could split your sides

The following day I didn't even try to get in touch with Welker. Instead I turned my attention to the police investigation into his wife's murder.

"Of course we have a file on him. The Swiss sent us their final report, not to mention that we did our own bit of investigating. Just a minute." Chief Inspector Nägelsbach would usually have hesitated a little longer before letting me peek into a file. "By the way, have you noticed any changes here?" he asked after he returned with the file.

I looked at him and then glanced around the room. There was a pile of sealed boxes beneath the window. "Are you moving?"

"I'm heading home. I'm gathering everything that belongs to me that I'll be taking along. I'm retiring."

I shook my head in disbelief.

He laughed. "I am. I'll be sixty-two this April. When the government came up with the pension-at-sixty-two plan my wife made me promise I'd stop working then. Starting next week I'll be taking all the vacation days I have coming. There you go." He pushed the folder across the desk toward me.

I began to read. Bertram and Stephanie Welker were seen together for the last time the morning they climbed up to the hut above the Roseg Glacier. On the afternoon of the following day Welker turned up alone at the Coaz chalet below the glacier. That morning he had found a note from his wife saying she was out hiking on the glacier and would meet up with him at eleven o'clock, halfway up the path he intended to take around the glacier. He had set out right away, at first waited for her at the halfway mark, and then ventured out onto the glacier, where he started looking for her. Finally he made his way as fast as he could down to the chalet and called the rescue service. The search went on for a number of weeks.

"How can one not find a body on a glacier?" I asked Nägelsbach.

"On a glacier? You mean *in* a glacier. She must have fallen into one of the countless crevasses, and since no one knew exactly where she'd been hiking, they couldn't look for her in a specific area, as they would have in other cases."

"What a gruesome idea: the woman lies buried in the ice, her youth and beauty preserved, and when they find her someday in the distant future, her aged husband is called in to identify her."

"My wife said that, too. She says something like that happens in some novel. But who's to say it will happen? Think of the Stone Age mummy from the Ötztal Alps, or Hannibal's soldiers, or those of the German emperors, or General Souvarov. Think of the Bernadine monks and all the early British mountain climbers. They were lost in the glaciers a lot longer than Frau Welker and have yet to be found."

I'd never seen my old friend like this. I must have stared at him in surprise.

"What you want to know is whether I think he murdered her. The fact that he had her note means nothing. There was no date on it, so it could be old. That he was at his wit's end when he turned up at the chalet doesn't mean anything, either. One would have to be quite a monster not to be a nervous wreck after killing one's own wife. What's in his favor is that one can't be sure a glacier near Saint Moritz would be free of hikers, even early in the morning. Pushing one's wife into a crevasse in the glacier is about as discreet as pushing her off a bridge onto an autobahn."

"If there's enough money at stake—"

"One takes bigger risks, I know. But then both had made more than enough money since their takeover of the Sorbian Cooperative Bank."

"Since what?"

"After the Berlin Wall fell, the Weller and Welker bank took over the Sorbian Cooperative Bank, a former East German institution based in Cottbus, with local branches nearby. The takeover was a success, not to mention that every investment people make now is supported by more grants than you can mention, all the way from Berlin to Brussels."

"But a man might also be ready to take a bigger risk when love or hatred—"

45

"No, there was no sign at all that he might have had a mistress, or she a lover. The two of them had been in love since they were children, and they were happily married. Have you seen pictures of her? A dark beauty, with eyes full of fire and spirit. It's true that beautiful women—and especially beautiful women—get murdered. But not by happy, loving husbands."

"Brigitte thinks she might have run away."

"My wife suggested that, too." He laughed. "What we have here is a touch of feminine instinct. Yes, she could have run away."

I waited to hear how the police followed up that lead and what they'd found, what his view of the likelihood of such a possibility was. When he said nothing, I asked him outright.

"She could be God knows where. It might not be the most charming way to leave a man, but then, no way of leaving someone is charming."

I'd known Nägelsbach since he had started working as a bailiff at the Heidelberg public prosecutor's office. He is a quiet, serious, thoughtful police officer. His hobby is building matchstick sculptures, models ranging from the Cologne Cathedral and Neuschwanstein Castle to the Bruchsal prison. He is often in a good mood and likes a good joke. Dark humor, satire, and sarcasm are foreign to him.

"What's wrong?" I asked.

He avoided my eyes and looked out the window. The trees were still bare, but their buds were on the verge of bursting open. He raised his hands and let them fall again. "I'm up for the Federal Cross of Merit."

"Well, congratulations!"

"Congratulations? It's true I was delighted at first. But . . ." He took a deep breath. "We've got this new chief. One of those energetic, efficient young men. Needless to say, he doesn't know us like the old chief did. But he's not particularly interested in us, either. So he walks up to me and says: 'Herr Nägelsbach, you'll be getting a Federal Cross of Merit when you leave. I'll be needing a few pages on you.' 'What for?' I asked. 'I don't know anything about you, but I'm sure you know all there is to know. I want you to write down for me why you deserve the ribbon in your buttonhole.' Can you imagine?"

"That's what new young bosses are like nowadays."

"I told him there was no way I'd do that, to which he replied that it was an official order."

"And?"

"He just laughed and went on his way."

"The 'official order' bit is just a silly joke."

"The whole thing's a silly joke. Federal Crosses of Merit, official orders, the years I sat here, the cases I worked on: so funny, you could split your sides. I realized that much too late. If I had realized it earlier I could have had a lot more fun."

"Haven't we always known that?"

"Known what?" He was hurt and defensive.

"That we could have had more fun in life."

"But . . ." He didn't go on. He looked out at the trees again, then at his desk, then at me. The hint of a smile flitted over his mouth. "Yes, perhaps I have always known it." He pushed his chair back and got up. "I've got to head out. Did you jot down old Herr Weller's address? The Augustinum retirement home in Emmertsgrund. The other parents are dead. By the way, he doesn't have Alzheimer's. He just sometimes acts like he does when you ask him a question he doesn't like."

11

Quick cash

Emmertsgrund, Heidelberg's newest residential development, lies on a slope above Leimen. The attractive apartments of the Augustinum retirement home face westward and have a view of the Rhine plain, just as the beautiful hospital rooms of the Speyerer Hof Clinic do. A cement factory lies at the foot of the hill, emitting pale, fine dust.

Old Herr Weller and I sat by the window. The two rooms of his apartment were filled with his own furniture, and before we sat down he told me the story of every piece. He also told me about his neighbors, with whom he didn't get along; the food there, which he didn't like; and the roster of social activities from folk dancing to silk painting, in which he wasn't interested. His failing eyesight prevented him from driving, so he was stuck in the Augustinum and felt lonely. I don't think he really believed that I was collecting donations for the German War Graves Commission, but he was lonely enough not to care who I was. What's more, we'd been both wounded in action in the Poland Campaign back in the war.

I invented a son, a daughter-in-law, and a grandson, and he told me about his family, and about the death of his daughter.

"Don't your son-in-law and grandchildren come to see you?" I asked him.

"He hasn't come since Stephanie died. I don't hold it against him, but he does have a bad conscience. As for my grandkids, they're off at school in Switzerland."

"Why should he have a bad conscience?"

"He should have looked after her. And he shouldn't have gone in for all that nonsense with that former East German bank."

While old Herr Weller had been complaining about his living conditions, there was a hint of whining in his voice. Now he spoke resolutely, and I felt the authority he must have once commanded.

"I thought it was all milk and honey with those banks in our new eastern states," I said.

"Let me tell you something, young man"—he was my age, but to my amazement actually addressed me as "young man"—"you don't have a background in banking, so I don't expect you to know any of this. The reason our bank survived was because it downsized, not because it expanded. We manage fortunes, advise investors, supervise funds, and do all that on a high international level. The few local people in Schwetzingen who still have accounts with us don't really fit the profile anymore. We serve them for old times' sake. And the clients of the Sorbian Cooperative Bank don't fit the profile, either, even if there are a lot of them; even if little and often fills the purse."

"Your son-in-law doesn't see eye-to-eye with you on this?"

"Him?" he bleated, laughing abruptly and contemptuously. "I've no idea what he can see, or if he can see at all, for that matter. He's a talented boy, but the bank's not his thing and never has been. He studied medicine, and old Welker ought to have let him become a doctor instead of forcing him into banking because of family tradition—as if things as they now stand still have anything to do with family tradition! It's all about fast money, new friends, new employees—I've no idea if the investment and funds business still exists the way Welker and I set it up. That's how far things have come: I have no idea what's going on."

Before I left he showed me a picture of his daughter. She was not the opulent beauty I'd imagined from seeing the photograph of her grandaunt at Schuler's place, or from Nägelsbach's description. She had a slender face, straight dark hair, and stern lips, and though her eyes had fire and soul, they also had an alert intelligence. "She was a banker and had studied law. She inherited the sixth sense for finances that our family developed over the centuries. If she were still alive the bank wouldn't be in the state it's in." He took his out wallet and gave me fifty marks. "For the war graves."

I drove home by way of Schwetzingen. The waitress at the café greeted me as an old regular. It was three thirty: time for a hot chocolate and a marble cake, and the end of a Friday workday at the Weller & Welker bank. At four o'clock the four young women emerged from the bank. They stood there for a moment and said good-bye to one another, and then two went off along the old moat, the other two in the direction of the train station. At four thirty the three young men appeared and went along the moat in the opposite direction. I left a twenty-mark bill on the table, waved to the waitress, and followed them. They walked quite a distance, past Messplatz and under the railroad tracks to an area where there was a car wash, a home-improvement outlet, and a liquor store. They went into an eight-story hotel and I could see them being given room keys at the front desk.

Back at the office, the light on my answering machine was blinking. Babs's son, Georg, had found my message and wanted to drop by: Would Sunday or Monday be better for me? Brigitte wanted us to go to the movies Saturday evening. The third call was from Schuler. "I'm sorry if I was a bit abrupt on the phone. I've had a chat with Bertram and Gregor, and I know now that you didn't say anything bad about me. It turns out Bertram has had a little too much on his plate of late, but he'll be dropping by later. Come and see me again: Perhaps next week? Maybe Monday?" He laughed, but it was not a joyful laugh. "There's life in the old badger yet. He's caught himself a fat goose."

12

Chock-full

That weekend spring assured us it meant business, that it had come to stay and would not be chased away by any more ice or snow. In the Luisenpark the deck chairs were out on the lawns, and I was dozing away, wrapped in a blanket as if all was well with the world and my heart was sound. Later, when Brigitte and I came out of the movie theater, the full moon lit up the streets and squares. Some punks were playing soccer with a beer can in the pedestrian zone, some bums were passing a bottle of wine around in front of the town hall, and couples were making out under the arbors of the Rosengarten.

"I'm looking forward to summer," Brigitte said, putting her arm around me.

On Sunday I had lunch with Georg in the Kleiner Rosengarten. He said he was willing to go to Strasbourg to search for the silent partner in old registries and telephone directories, the records of legal and notary chambers, and lecture schedules. He was ready to leave on Monday. I appointed him assistant detective and ordered champagne, but he wanted to stick to alcohol-free beer.

"You drink too much, Uncle Gerhard."

That evening I was back in my office poring over the history of banking. The Sorbian Cooperative Bank also had a paragraph dedicated to it. It was a rarity. Cooperative banks had actually come about as self-help establishments set up by occupational groups. Schulze-Delitzsch had set out to make artisans into members of a cooperative through cooperative banks, while Raiffeisen strove to do the same with farmers. Hans Kleiner from Cottbus, who founded the Sorbian Cooperative Bank in 1868, wanted to inspire cooperative ideas in the Sorbian Slavic minority. His mother was Sorbian, wore Sorbian dress, told little Hans Sorbian fairy tales and taught him Sorbian songs, with the result that he made Sorbian affairs his life's work. During his lifetime the bank had only Sorbian members, but after his death it opened its doors to others, expanded, flourished, and survived the great inflation and the worldwide depression. Then came a great blow. The Nazis wanted nothing to do with the Sorbians and turned the bank into a regular cooperative bank.

When and how the Sorbian Cooperative Bank was to recover from this blow would have to wait till tomorrow. Weller & Welker had taken the bank over, so it must have recovered and had a happy ending. On my way home that night I found the cooperative idea so sensible that the usual hankering of banks and bankers for more and more money suddenly struck me as strange. Why heap money upon money? Because a child's compulsion to collect things can in adult years no longer be satisfied by collecting marbles, beer coasters, and stamps, and so must turn to money?

The following morning I was sitting once more at the desk in my office before the children of the neighborhood were heading to school. The bakery a few doors down was already open, and a steaming cup of coffee and a croissant stood before me. There wasn't much more to the story of the Sorbian Cooperative Bank. While other such banks were closed down by the Soviets, those in and around Cottbus continued to be run under the name of Sorbian Cooperative Bank. The bank was completely absorbed into the system of a state-owned savings bank. Yet it did keep its name; respect for the Sorbian Slavic people, brothers of the victorious Soviet people, forbade its abolition. Along with its name it also kept sufficient autonomy for the Treuhand Agency, formed after the reunification of Germany to privatize East German enterprises, to put the Sorbian Cooperative Bank on the market, ultimately selling it to Weller & Welker.

It was nine o'clock and the morning traffic on the Augusta-anlage had quieted down. I heard children, who for some reason or other didn't have to get to school till later. Then I heard a car pull up by the sidewalk, where it stopped with its engine running. The rattling and chugging began to get on my nerves after a while. Why didn't they turn the engine off? I got up and looked out the window.

It was Schuler's green Isetta. Its door was clapped open, but the car was empty. I went out onto the sidewalk. Schuler was standing in the entrance next door, reading the names beside the buzzers.

"Herr Schuler!" I called, and he turned and waved. He waved as if he were shooing me away from the sidewalk—as if he wanted me to get back into my office. I didn't understand, and though he seemed to be calling out something to me I couldn't hear him. He came staggering toward me, his right hand still waving, his left hand pressed to his stomach. I could see that his left hand was holding the handle of a black attaché case that was knocking against his legs. I took a few steps toward him and he bumped into me. I got a whiff of his bad smell and heard him whisper "Take this!" and "Go!" He shoved the case toward me and I took it. He steadied himself on me with the hand that had just given me the case and righted himself. He hurried over to his car, got in, closed the door, and drove off.

He swerved in a crooked line from the sidewalk to the right lane, and then from the right lane into the left. He steered toward the steel bollards bordering the traffic island in the middle of the Augustaanlage, scraped one, scraped the next, scraped the traffic light at Mollstrasse, and picked up speed without paying any attention to the light, which had turned red, to the cars that had just started entering from Mollstrasse, or to the children who had begun crossing the Augustaanlage. At first it looked as if he would crash into the lights or the tree at the edge of the island on the other side of Mollstrasse. But he rolled over the curb, missed the lights, and grazed the tree lightly, and yet the curb and the tree tilted the Isetta enough to capsize it, sending it sliding on its side over the grass until it crashed into another tree.

It was a loud crash, and at the same moment, in the opposite lane, into which the Isetta had almost careened, brakes screeched and drivers he had cut off blew their horns. A child over whose feet he'd almost skidded began to bawl. All hell broke loose. My Turkish neighbor came hurrying out of his store, took the attaché case from me, and said: "Go see if he's all right. I'll call the police and an ambulance." I hurried over, but I'm not as quick as I used to be, and by the time I got to the Isetta a crowd of onlookers had already gathered. I pushed my way forward. The tree had crushed the door and was lodged between the roof and floor of the car. I looked down through the side window: the car was full of glass and blood, the crushed door had pinned Schuler back into the seat, and the wheel was jammed into his chest. He was dead.

The police and ambulance arrived and, as they could not pry the Isetta loose from the tree, the fire department was brought in. The police made no sign of taking a statement from me, and I did not come forward to present myself as a witness. I headed back to my office, the front door of which I'd left open. From a distance I saw someone leave my office. I couldn't imagine what he'd be doing there, or what he might be looking for. Nothing was missing.

My Turkish neighbor's store experienced a mini-boom. The onlookers were watching the goings-on surrounding the Isetta, offering expert commentary, and buying candy, chocolate, and granola bars.

It was only when everything was over and things had calmed down that I remembered Schuler's attaché case. I picked it up from the Turk, placed it on my desk, and eyed it. Black matte faux leather, a gold-colored combination lock—an ugly, run-of-the-mill attaché case. From my desk I took out the bottle of Sambuca and the box of coffee beans I kept there, poured myself a drink, and dropped three beans into the glass. I found a package of Sweet Aftons in the filing cabinet and lit both—the Sambuca and the cigarette—and watched the blue flames and blue smoke.

I thought of Schuler. I'd have liked to hear him once again tell his tales: why Lieutenant Welker and the Prussian had gotten into an argument, what had been the fate of the young Weller girl after her beloved had met his death, much like Romeo—except that in this case the families were not hostile to each other, but too friendly. I would have liked to have known when Bertram and Stephanie had fallen in love. I blew out the flame and drank. I wished Schuler could have recovered his sense of taste and smell before he died.

Then I opened the attaché case. It was chock-full of money, used fifty- and hundred-mark bills.

13

Shadowed

No, I didn't consider stuffing the bills into a suitcase along with a few shirts and pants, sweaters, underwear, toothbrush, and razor, heading to the Frankfurt airport, and getting on the first plane to Buenos Aires. Or the Maldives, the Azores, or the Hebrides. My life here in Mannheim is complicated enough. How would it be someplace else, where I don't even speak the language?

I didn't look for a hiding place for the money, either. As it is, I would surely tell all under torture. I lowered the rolltop of my filing cabinet, squeezed the few old files into one of its compartments, and slid out the bottoms of the other compartments, making enough space for the attaché case. Then I pulled the rolltop shut.

I didn't count the money. There was a lot of it. Enough to give someone reason to put the fear of God into a man. Thinking of my final meeting with Schuler on the sidewalk— the way he staggered toward me waving his arms, his grimacing, his hoarse whisper—I felt that someone must have frightened him to death.

Nägelsbach sounded no happier on the phone than he'd been when I had seen him.

"What was it, an accident or a murder?" he asked me. "As you know, each has its own department."

"All I want to know is when Schuler's body will be sent over to Forensics."

"Yes, I know, so you can call your friend at the Mannheim municipal hospital, who'll then put in a quick call to Forensics. By the way, what are you doing . . . I mean, on Tuesday . . . my wife . . . you see . . . tomorrow's my last day, and we would be delighted if you and your girlfriend would come by. Are you free?"

He sounded worried that nobody would come to his party. He and his wife struck me as never really needing friends, as if they were quite self-sufficient, and there were times when I envied that. They'd sit in his workshop, he working on a matchstick model of the Munich Palace of Justice, she reading aloud to him from Kafka's *The Trial*, and before bed they'd have a glass of wine together. Does marital harmony last only till retirement?

As I drove to Schwetzingen I was shadowed. Even as I walked to my car, just around the corner from my office, I had the feeling that someone was following me. But whenever I turned around nobody was there, and such feelings can be wrong, even if Brigitte believes that feelings always tell the truth and that only thoughts tell lies. There wasn't much traffic on the autobahn. The beige Fiesta I noticed in my rearview mirror after the Mannheim intersection passed me when I pulled over on the shoulder near Pfingstberg, drove on, and disappeared from view around the next bend. But when I drove on and then passed a truck and looked into my rearview mirror, there it was again. I repeated my little maneuver a few hundred yards from the Schwetzingen exit. When he passed me I tailed him until he took the exit. I drove on and then, a few kilometers beyond Brühl, pulled over the shoulder onto a bumpy dirt road.

I was not surprised to find a police car outside Schuler's place. No one was parked outside the old warehouse. I rang and managed to get in, but I couldn't open the door to the archives. When I drove off, I once again saw the Fiesta in my rearview mirror.

I felt tired—tired of a world in which a harmless, malodorous old archivist could at the drop of a hat be frightened to death. A world in which there were too many used fifty- and hundred-mark bills. In which someone could snoop about in my office and shadow me in a beige Fiesta without my knowing who he was and what he wanted. I felt tired of being at odds with my case. It didn't interest me and couldn't interest my client, either. What interested me instead was my client himself, and the death of his wife and his archivist. And that I was interested in this was, needless to say, of no interest to my client. But what was his interest? And why had he hired me for a case that surely could not be of interest to him?

The message on my answering machine sounded as if Welker had read my mind. "Hello, Herr Self. Can you drop by tomorrow? I haven't heard from you in a while and would like an update. As things stand, time's not on our side, and . . ." He covered the mouthpiece and there was a sound on the line like in the shell from the Timmendorf beach in which my mother had me listen to the sea when I was a little boy. In between I heard mumbled words that I couldn't make out. Then Samarin came on the line: "We know that Herr Schuler came to see you, and that he left some money with you. You must help us see to it that his reputation isn't ruined by this one foolish act. The money belongs back in the bank. Come by tomorrow at three."

I was tired of the game Welker and Samarin were playing. I didn't call either of them. I decided to call Georg the following day in Strasbourg to see what he'd come up with. I also decided to call Nägelsbach on his last day at police headquarters. I had forgotten that I had been shadowed by a Fiesta.

14

Not empty-handed

But the driver of the Fiesta had not forgotten me. At eight thirty the following morning he was at my front door, ringing the bell. He rang many times. Later he explained to me that he had been quite considerate; he had kept ringing even though he could have easily gotten the door open. The lock was a joke.

When I opened, he stood there skulking like a salesman, his face both defiant and dispirited. He looked to be about fifty, not too tall and not too short, not fat and not thin, his cheeks covered in spider veins and his hair sparse. He was wearing pants of some dark synthetic fabric, light gray loafers, a light blue shirt with dark blue edging on the pocket, and an open parka. His parka was the same beige color as his car.

"So it was you," I said.

"Me?"

"Who was shadowing me yesterday."

He nodded. "That maneuver of yours near Schwetzingen wasn't bad, but I knew where you were heading. You went off the autobahn just like that? Over the shoulder and onto a dirt road?" He spoke with magnanimous amiability. "What about the blue Mercedes? Did it follow you onto the dirt road?"

I didn't want to let on that I had no idea what he was talking about, but he saw that right away.

"Are you telling me you didn't notice him? As for me, you only noticed yesterday."

"I'd be happy enough not to notice you today, either. What do you want?"

He looked hurt. "Why are you talking to me like that? I didn't do anything to you. I just wanted—"

"Well?"

"You are . . . I am . . ."

I waited.

"You are my father."

I'm not the fastest person and never have been, and with the passing years I haven't gotten any faster. More often than not my emotions are slow to react, and I might notice only at noon that someone had offended me in the morning, or I might realize in the evening that someone had said something nice to me at lunch that would have pleased me. I don't have a son. And yet I didn't burst out laughing or slam the door in his face, but invited him into my living room and had him sit on one sofa while I sat on the other.

"You don't believe me?" he said, and then nodded. "I see you don't believe me. We don't even exist for you."

"We? How many more children do I have?"

"There's no need to make fun of me." He told me that he had seen his file after the fall of the Berlin Wall and had discovered that he had been adopted, and that his real mother was Klara Self from Berlin.

"What file was this?"

"My cadre file."

"Cadre . . . ?"

"I worked for the Stasi—the East German secret services—and am proud of it. I investigated serious crimes, and I'll have you know that our total of solved cases was higher than you here in the West could ever hope for. Things weren't all bad in East Germany, and I won't have it or me painted black."

I motioned to him to calm down. "When were you born?"

"March ninth, 1942. Your fascist Wehrmacht was attacking the Soviet Union."

I did my arithmetic. March 9, 1942, I was living at the hotel in Heidelberg, behind me the Poland Campaign, getting wounded in action, and the field hospital. I had finished my law degree and begun working at the public prosecutor's office. I had not yet found an apartment, so Klara was staying with her parents in Berlin. Or was she traveling with her girl-friend Gigi through Italy? Or was she somewhere in hiding so she could give birth to a child? I would have liked to have had children. But not a child born on March 9, 1942. From May to August 1941, I was in Warthegau and had been with Klara only a single night.

I shook my head. "I'm sorry, but—"

"I knew it. I knew you'd shake your head and say, 'I'm sorry, I don't want to have anything to do with you.' You could talk about us as brothers and sisters. That you could do, but you could never act like we were. There you shake your head and raise your hands." He shook his head and raised his hands, the way he imagined us doing. He was trying to sound derisive but in fact sounded despondent.

I shouldn't have told him that I was sorry. I was not sorry that I wasn't his father. Furthermore, my apology provoked more accusations, which again triggered my apology reflex. I was on the point of apologizing for all the rigors the West did and did not unleash upon the East.

"I'm not coming empty-handed. You didn't notice the blue Mercedes when you were driving to Schwetzingen, and I imagine you didn't notice it this morning, either." He saw the interest in my face. "You want to know more. Well, I'll tell you more. The Mercedes came after the old man gave you the attaché case and got into his car. It pulled up, and during the brouhaha the man sitting next to the driver got out and went snooping, first around your office and then around the old man's car. I needn't tell you what he was looking for."

"Do you know who these men were?"

"All I know is that the Mercedes's number plates were from Berlin. But I'll find out. As it is, you and I are in the same line of business, and soon you'll be . . . soon enough you'll be . . ." He fell silent.

He actually was thinking of taking over my business, from father to son. Not right away, but after a period of transition in which we would operate as "Detective Agency: Gerhard Self & Son." I did not propose "Gerhard Self & Klara Self's Son." I didn't explain to him that he might possibly be the son of my deceased wife, but that he was most definitely no son of mine. I didn't want to confide in him, talking about my marriage, opening up about myself, compromising Klara. In later years our marriage had been empty. But in those early days, when I had started at the Heidelberg public prosecutor's office and Klara was soon to follow me to Heidelberg, our marriage was young and, I thought, full of magic, promising lasting happiness. It did affect me that there might have been someone else with whom Klara had had a relationship and a child, someone who didn't even love her enough to insist she divorce me and marry him. Or did he die on the battlefield? I recalled an officer she knew, about whom she initially spoke a lot but then stopped mentioning, an officer who fell outside Moscow. I searched the face of the man before me for that officer's features but found no trace of them.

"What is your name?"

"Karl-Heinz Ulbrich, with a hyphen. The Ulbrich without a *T*."

"Where do you live?"

"At the Kolpinghaus. Its address is R 7—isn't that crazy? That sounds like . . . like a cigarette brand name, not a street." He shook his head in disbelief.

I forbore explaining the Mannheim street system. I also didn't ask him whether he wasn't ashamed as an old Communist to be staying at the Kolpinghaus.

As if all this wasn't bad enough, Turbo returned from one of his forays over the rooftops, jumped from the windowsill onto the sofa, and rubbed against Karl-Heinz Ulbrich's legs on his way to the kitchen. Karl-Heinz said "puss-puss," his eyes following Turbo with satisfaction. He looked at me triumphantly, as if he'd always known that animals in the West were friendlier than people and that this had now been proven. Luckily he didn't say this out loud.

He got up. "I guess I'd better go. But I'll be back."

Without waiting for a good-bye, he walked through the hall to the door, opened it, and from outside carefully closed it again.

15

Without confession there is no absolution

I called Strasbourg. I couldn't get hold of Georg—though after he'd been there just a day he wouldn't have had much to report. So I had to make do with what Schuler had told me.

The silent partner from Strasbourg whose first or last name bore the initial *C*, *L*, or *Z* seemed to spark little interest in Welker or Samarin. As I sat opposite them making my report, Samarin looked visibly bored, while Welker seemed to be trying to suppress his impatience.

I'd said all I had to say. "I've picked up the Strasbourg lead and can either follow it or drop it. I do get the impression, however, that you've lost interest in the silent partner."

Welker assured me that the silent partner was as important

to him as ever. "Let me write you another check. Strasbourg won't be a cheap venture."

He took his checkbook and a fountain pen out of his jacket and wrote me a check.

"Herr Self," Samarin said, leaning forward and looking me in the eye. "It seems that Schuler had access to the bank and withdrew some money. He left that money with you, and—"

"He brought me an attaché case, which I have placed in the care of a third party. I'm not sure whether I should hand it over to his heirs or the police. I don't even know who his heirs are, or the exact circumstances of Schuler's death."

"He died in a car crash."

"Somebody frightened him to death," I countered.

Samarin shook his head—slowly, ponderously—and as he did so he rocked his upper body back and forth. "Herr Self." He squeezed out the words. "When someone takes something that doesn't belong to him, it doesn't do that person any good."

"Gentlemen, gentlemen," Welker said soothingly, glancing at Samarin and me with some irritation as he handed me the check. "You must understand that decades ago Herr Schuler was our teacher, a good teacher, and we don't forget it. His death was a blow to us, and the suspicion about the money, too. I must say that I cannot believe—"

Samarin exploded. "You *will* believe what—"

"What you tell me?" Welker looked at Samarin and me triumphantly for a few seconds.

Samarin was so furious that he almost tipped the heavy chair over as he got up. But he managed to get a grip on himself. Slowly and menacingly he said, "You will be hearing from me, Herr Self."

I walked along the palace gardens to Schuler's house. I

couldn't figure out what Welker's moment of triumph was all about. Or why the money that had disappeared seemed to worry him less than it worried Samarin. If there was something fishy about the used fifty- and hundred-mark bills, whether Schuler had taken them or not, then this ought to worry the boss more than his assistant, even if his assistant is responsible for practical matters and has a tendency to be overbearing and is quick to flare up. Or were they playing some version of the good-cop, bad-cop routine with me? But if that were the case, Samarin could have exploded instead of getting a grip on himself.

I looked around but nobody was following me, neither my counterfeit son nor a blue Mercedes. The woman who opened the door at Schuler's house was his niece. She had been crying and again burst into tears the moment she began to speak. "He smelled and grouched and nagged. But he was such a good person, such a good person. Everyone knew it, and his students liked him and came to see him, and he helped them every way he could."

She herself had been a student of his, as had her husband. They met when both happened to drop by one day to see Schuler.

We sat in the kitchen, which she had tidied up a little. She had made some tea and offered me a cup. "There's no sugar. When it came to sugar, I managed to talk some sense into him. As for alcohol, he wouldn't listen." The thought of this brought more tears to her eyes. "He wasn't long for this world, but that doesn't make it any better. Do you know what I mean? It doesn't make it any better."

"What do the police say?"

"The police?"

I told her that her uncle's accident had happened right out-side my door. "I came to Schwetzingen right away to inform you, but the police were already here."

"Yes, the precinct in Mannheim called our local station, and they came by. It was a coincidence that I happened to be here. I don't come every day. He wants . . . I mean, he wanted . . ." Again she began to cry.

"Did the police say anything, or ask you anything?"

"No."

"Your uncle was in a terrible state when he came to see me right before his accident. It was as if he'd suffered a shock, as if something had really frightened him."

"Why did you let him drive?" She looked at me reproach-fully through her tears.

"It all happened much too fast. Your uncle . . . He was here one minute, gone the next."

"But surely you could have held him back, I mean you could have . . ." She pulled out a handkerchief and blew her nose. "I'm sorry. I know how difficult he could be once he'd gotten something into his head. And here I am, practically accusing you. I didn't mean to." She looked at me sadly, but I reproached myself with everything she wasn't reproaching me with. She was right: Why hadn't I held him back? Why didn't I at least try? This time it wasn't only my emotions that had been too slow.

"I . . ." But I didn't know what to say. I looked at her as she sat bent forward, her hands weakly clasping the handker-chief, her face warm, innocent. She hadn't asked me who I was, but had simply taken me for a friend of her uncle's, a companion in grief. I felt as if I'd not only let Schuler down, but her as well, and I sought absolution in her face. But I could find none. Without confession there is no absolution.

16

No class

When Brigitte and I arrived at the retirement party the Nägelsbachs were throwing at their place in the Pfaffengrund settlement, Nägelsbach was already tipsy and morosely cheerful.

"Well, Herr Self? At first my colleagues didn't want to hand your friend over to Forensics, but I had a word with them and they finally sent him over. Speaking of which, from now on you'll have to make do on your own. I won't be able to help you anymore."

His wife took Brigitte and me aside. "His boss asked me what kind of present he might like," she said. "I'm afraid he's thinking of turning up here uninvited. If he does come, can you intercept him? I don't want him suddenly coming face-to-face with my husband."

She was wearing a long black gown—I couldn't tell if it was for mourning at the end of her husband's career, or because it was beautiful and suited her, or if she wanted to portray somebody: Virginia Woolf, Juliette Gréco, or Charlotte Corday on her way to the scaffold. She does things like that.

The guests were crowded into the dining area and living room, which were connected by an open sliding door. I greeted this and that police officer I recognized from the Heidelberg headquarters. Brigitte whispered to me: "Forensics? Did he just mention forensics? Do you have anything to do with forensics?"

Frau Nägelsbach brought us two glasses of apricot punch.

The doorbell kept ringing, and guests kept arriving. The hall door stood open and I heard a voice I recognized. "No, I'm not a guest. I'm with Herr Self and need to speak to him." It was Karl-Heinz Ulbrich, wearing a beige anorak over a white nylon shirt and a flowery tie. He came straight over to me, took me by the arm, and steered me through the hall into the empty kitchen.

"It's the Russians," he whispered, as if they were standing right next to him and might overhear.

"Who?"

"The men in the bank and the blue Mercedes. Russians, or Chechens, or Georgians, or Azerbaijanis." He looked at me meaningfully and expectantly.

"And?"

"You really don't know?" he asked, shaking his head. "They're not to be trifled with. The Russian Mafia's nothing like what you've got here in the West—nothing like the Italians or Turks. The Russians are brutal."

"You're saying this as if you were proud."

"You must take precautions. When they want something, they get it. Whatever's in that attaché case, it's not worth crossing them."

Was he puffing himself up? Or was he one of them, whoever *they* might be? Were they the rough guys, while he was sent to soften me up, all in an attempt to get back the attaché case?

"What's in the attaché case?" I asked him.

He stared at me despondently. "How are we to work together if you don't trust me? Not to mention, how do you expect to get through this if we don't work together?"

Brigitte came into the kitchen. "His boss has arrived, and Frau Nägelsbach . . ."

But it was already too late. We heard Nägelsbach greeting his boss with exaggerated civility. Would he like a glass of punch? Or perhaps two or three? Some situations are bearable only with alcohol. Some people, too.

Brigitte and I went into the living room, though Ulbrich still kept after me. As a good-bye present Nägelsbach's boss had brought him a photograph of the Heidelberg police headquarters, as if it were the Grand Hotel, and he was doing his best to be pleasant, unaware of the emotions he was triggering. I started chatting with him about the police in different parts of the country and the secret services, and judging by the things he said, he knew a thing or two. I asked him about the Russian Mafia but he shrugged his shoulders. "Do you know what someone from RTL Television said to me the other day? All the private stations are scouring material for

TV, but one thing you can't offer the public is the Russian Mafia. Not because it doesn't exist. The thing is, it has no class, no style, no tradition, no religion—none of the things one likes about the Italians. All the Russian Mafia has is brutality." He shook his head in disappointment. "In this case, too, Communism has steamrolled over culture."

By the time Brigitte and I headed back home, Ulbrich had disappeared. I hoped it was the headlights of his Fiesta that I saw in my rearview mirror. If not, they now knew about Brigitte.

17

The black attaché case

I lay awake that night. Should I give Samarin the black attaché case? Or should I give it to the police, making certain that the men in the blue Mercedes followed me to the station and saw what I did? Or should I put it by the lamppost outside my office while they were parked a few cars away and wait for them to get out, pick it up, and drive off—out of my life?

When I called Nägelsbach in the morning, he was hungover. It wasn't easy to explain to him what I intended to do. When he finally understood, he was appalled. "You want to do that at the Heidelberg police headquarters? Where all my life I—" He hung up. Half an hour later he called back. "Okay, we can do that at the headquarters in Mannheim. They know me, and there'll be no problem with me parking there for a while. Did you say at five?"

"Yes, and could you please thank your wife for me?"

He laughed. "She put in a good word for you."

I packed only a few things. It all had to fit in the black attaché case. I didn't need a lot; it wouldn't take more than a couple of days.

Turbo sensed that I was going away. The neighbors would look after him, but he pouted and disappeared, as children do when they realize that Mom and Dad are about to go on a trip.

I took my things and dropped in at Brigitte's massage practice at the Collini-Center. I had to wait, so I read an article in an old magazine about a movie set in East Germany before reunification: a young couple set out on heists in Bonnie-and-Clyde fashion, robbing the old-style, vulnerable banks of the new currency that had just been introduced. Until they got too wild and began robbing banks in Berlin and got shot.

Brigitte saw her patient off and sat down next to me. "I'm expecting the next client any minute, and thank God for that, because the health-care reform has cost me a third of my old patients, and finding new ones who'll come in even though their insurance won't reimburse them isn't easy."

I nodded.

"What's going on?"

"I'll be away for a few days. My case has ground to a halt. I might be able to get it going again someplace else. Not to mention that I feel a bit spooky around here. If anyone asks for me, you can tell them that."

She got up with a hurt look. "I know the script well enough: '*What's going on?*' *she asks him.* '*Nothing,*' *he* replies, looking out the window into the twilight with a stony glare. Then he turns and looks deep into her eyes. 'It's better this way, honey. The less you know, the better. I don't want the guys to get on your case, too.'"

"Come on, Brigitte. I'll tell you all about it when I get back. Believe me, I don't want to hide anything from you. But right now it's better if you don't know what's going on. Believe me."

"'Trust me, my darling,' he tells her, looking at her intently. 'I've got to think for the two of us right now.'" The bell rang and Brigitte got up to open the door. "Well, take care of yourself!"

I found a place to park on the Augustaanlage, not far from my office. When I got out of the car I didn't see the blue Mercedes anywhere. Back at my office, I took out the black attaché case and emptied the bills into a trash bag. There was a large plant pot under my desk and a bag of soil that I had bought quite a while ago to replant my potted palm. I put the trash bag inside the new pot beneath the palm tree; the plant didn't get quite as much soil under its roots as I'd initially planned, but if it didn't like it, it could go to hell. I never liked that plant.

I put my overnight bag into the attaché case. When I left my office with it, the blue Mercedes was waiting on the other side of the street. The man beside the driver opened the door, got out, and came running toward me. By the time he made it across the street through the evening traffic I was already in my Opel, driving off. He waved to the Mercedes, which honked its horn and cut into traffic and made a U-turn to my side of the street at Werderstrasse, despite a red light. There it picked up the other man and tailed me through the Schwetzingerstadt district.

Mollstrasse, Seckenheimer Strasse, Heinrich-Lanz-Strasse—the streets were filled with cars and bicycles, the stores were open, the sidewalks were bustling, and children were playing in front of the Heilig-Geist Church. This was my safe everyday world. What could happen to me here? Yet the Mercedes was tailing me so closely that I couldn't see its grille in my rearview mirror but could clearly make out the humorless, set faces of the driver and the man beside him. In the Heinrich-Lanz Strasse he tapped me—a gentle meeting of his bumper with mine—and fear crept up my spine. When the light turned red at the Reichskanzler-Müller-Strasse and we stopped, the man got out of his car and walked up to my locked door, and I don't know what he would have done if a patrol car hadn't gone by and the light turned green.

In front of police headquarters I drove half up onto the sidewalk and, clutching the attaché case, was out of the car, up the stairs, and through the door before the man could even get out of the Mercedes. I leaned against the wall, hugging the attaché case to my chest and panting as if I'd run all the way from the Augustaanlage.

Nägelsbach was waiting in his Audi inside the yard of the police station. I gave him the attaché case and he put it on the floor by the front seat. Then he helped me climb into the trunk. "My wife's put a blanket in there—do you think you'll manage?"

When he let me out at the airport parking lot at Neuostheim, he was certain nobody had followed him. He was also certain that nobody had seen me climb out of the trunk.

"Do you want me to come along with you?"

"Are you already at loose ends at home, with all that free time on your hands?"

"Not at all. I've been conscripted into cleaning up after yesterday's party." But he stood there, hesitant and somewhat despondent. "Well, then."

A little later I was in the air, looking down at Mannheim, keeping my eyes peeled for beige Fiestas and blue Mercedes.

18

Fear of flying

The woman next to me was afraid of flying. She asked me to hold her hand, and I did. As we were taking off, I reassured her with the information that most airplane accidents occur not during takeoff but during landing. An hour and a half later, when our plane began to descend, I confessed that I had not been all that honest with her. The truth is that most airplane accidents do in fact occur during takeoff, not when the plane is landing. We had taken off quite a while ago, so she could sit back and relax. But she didn't, and at Berlin Tempelhof she rushed off without so much as a good-bye.

I hadn't been in Berlin since 1942, and I wouldn't have been tempted to come if the fastest route to Cottbus hadn't been by plane via Berlin. I knew that the five-story house in which I had grown up had been destroyed in 1945, along with all the neighboring houses, and replaced in the fifties by a six-story apartment block. My parents had died in the attack. Klara's parents had moved out of their villa near Wannsee to a villa on Lake Starnberg shortly before the end of the war. The friends of my childhood and youth had dispersed in all directions. In the seventies we had a class reunion. I didn't go. I don't want to remember.

I found a cheap hotel at the intersection of Friedrichstrasse and Unter den Linden. As I stood by the window, looking down at the traffic, I got the urge to go out and take a look around and perhaps find a restaurant where the food tastes like it used to, like it did at home. I went to the Brandenburg Gate, saw the buildings rising on the Pariser Platz, the cranes towering into the skies. On the Potsdamer Platz they had sawed open the city's torso and were conducting open heart surgery: floodlights, excavations, cranes, scaffolding, and building skeletons, sometimes already floor after floor with finished masonry, balconies, and windows. I walked on and recognized the Ministry of Aviation and the remains of the Anhalter train station, and on Tempelhofer Ufer the building where I had worked as a junior clerk for a lawyer. I avoided the street where I had been a child.

I didn't find a restaurant whose food promised to taste the way it used to. But I found an Italian restaurant where the perch and the crème caramel were the way they ought to be, and the carafe of Sardinian white wine overshadowed all the Frascati, suave, or pinot grigios. I was content, asked where the nearest metro station was, and set out for my hotel.

I wanted to transfer at the Hallesches Tor, but as I got off the last car I came face-to-face with seven or eight young men with shaved heads, black jackets, and military boots, standing there as if they'd been waiting for me.

"Hey! Granddad!"

I wanted to keep going but they wouldn't let me through, and when I tried to sidestep them they wouldn't let me pass. They forced me back toward the outer edge of the platform. The metro line here crosses the Landwehr Canal like an elevated railway, and I could see the dark water beneath me.

"Where are you heading, Grandpa?"

On the opposite platform I saw some youths who were looking at us with interest. Otherwise the platforms were empty. "To my hotel and to bed."

They laughed as if I'd just uttered the greatest one-liner. "To his hotel!" one of them hooted, leaning forward and slapping his thighs. "To bed!" Then he said: "You were there, right?"

"Where?"

"With the Führer, where else? Did you ever get to see him?"

I nodded.

"Give Grandpa some of your beer; he saw the Führer." The leader of the pack nudged the young man next to him, and he offered me his can of beer.

"Thank you, but I've already drunk enough this evening."

"Did you hear that? He got to see the Führer!" the leader announced to his pack; he also yelled it out to the youths on the opposite platform. Then he asked me: "And how did you greet him?"

"Come on, surely you know that."

"Show me, Grandpa!"

"I don't want to do that."

"You don't want to show us? Then do as I do!" He clicked his heels together, flung his right arm into the air, and yelled: "Heil Hitler!" The others didn't utter a sound. He brought his arm down. "So?"

"I don't want to."

"You'd rather take a swim down there?"

"No, I just want to go—to my hotel, and to bed."

This time nobody laughed. The leader came closer and I edged back until I felt the railing against my spine. He raised his hands and patted me down, as if he were searching for weapons. "You're not wearing a life jacket, Grandpa. You might drown. If you get water in your nose—" With a jolt he jammed his index and middle fingers into my nostrils and pushed my head backward until I was at the point of losing my balance. "So?" He let go of me.

My nose was smarting. I was frightened. I couldn't think fast enough: Should I play along? Would that be cleverer? Was that cowardly? Was it some sort of betrayal? Was this and what it symbolized worth getting hurt or getting pneumonia? They grabbed hold of me and I stuttered out a "Heil Hitler." The leader of the pack told me to say it louder and I said it louder, and when he again said, "Louder!" and they let go of me, I stood on the platform and shouted as loud as I could: "Heil Hitler!"

Now they were laughing again and clapping. "Bravo, Granddad! Bravo!" But their leader shook his head silently until all the others fell silent and then said: "He didn't raise his arm, though, did he? It doesn't count without the arm." They stared at him and then at me and then at him, and they understood before I did. They grabbed me by the arms and legs, hooted, and swung me back and forth—"one, two, three"—and as the metro came thundering into the station, they flung me over the railing into the canal. When I surfaced, I could still hear them hooting.

The stone embankment on the near side was too steep, but I made it to the other side and managed to climb onto the street across a wooden landing. Two taxis didn't stop, but the third driver had plastic covers on his seats, so twenty minutes later I was back at my hotel and under a hot shower.

I hadn't come to any great harm. The following morning, the side of my body that had hit the water was a single big bruise. I also had a runny nose and a slight fever. But my injury was elsewhere. I'd had a chance to make up for the wrongs I had done in the old days. And when does one ever get such a chance? But I'd done it wrong again.

19

Everything comes together

The Sorbian Cooperative Bank is on the old market square in Cottbus. I went inside and took a look around until I ran the risk of being noticed. Then I went to the teller and got 91.50 marks for the fifty-dollar bill I'd just purchased across the street at the Deutsche Bank for 99.50 marks.

It was like any other bank. The modern furnishings were of wood and steel, the walls covered with large abstract paintings. What was different was the life-sized wood relief of Hans Kleiner by the door, guarding the entrance. Also different was that Vera Soboda, the manager, had her desk right in the main hall, which was either a legacy of the Socialist past or state-of-the-art management and administration. If the woman sitting at the desk was Vera Soboda, then the Sorbian Cooperative Bank had a manager of middle years, somewhat plump, somewhat tough, more tractor driver on a Socialist farming cooperative than banker. But the staff going up to her from other desks interacted with her with such deference and speed that I concluded she must have given them the best of training.

In this bank, too, there was a gate on the side, but I didn't see any cars driving in or out, even though I lingered all day, frozen to the bone, in various stores, at an Eduscho café, and in doorways. I didn't see any young men in dark suits, either. The abundant bank clientele was made up of local people: modest savers, some in anoraks and gray loafers of the kind Karl-Heinz Ulbrich wore, some in bright and shiny tracksuits, some in pants and jackets that looked as if the blue of the East German Youth Movement shirts were vying for a second career in West European fashion.

The only remaining sign of East Germany was the people's clothes. The stores belonged to the same chains as those in Mannheim and Heidelberg, Viernheim and Schwetzingen. I looked into side streets and saw more streets that had just been dug up, more houses that were being renovated, sometimes also a house in a state of utter ruin. On the other hand, there were fewer of the architectural sins of the sixties and seventies. The housing projects I had seen as the train headed toward the station were no worse than those in Waldhof or Boxberg. Everything was coming together.

It rained in the afternoon. My nose was running and I felt feverish, so I got myself some medicine from a drugstore that turned my mucus membranes to parchment. But the people were different here: it wasn't only that they were wearing different, shabbier clothes. They also had different, wearier faces. They were slower, more hesitant and careful. There was none of that familiar cheeriness and resolve in their expressions and gestures. They reminded me of the old days. I saw my reflection in a storefront, shabby in my old, wet raincoat, my face tired, and any exertion seemed a strain. Was I more suited to the East than the West?

In the afternoon I managed to get hold of Georg in Strasbourg from a telephone booth outside the Sorbian Cooperative Bank. He had found a name: Paul Laban. The *L* was right, the dates were right, and as a professor at the University of Strasbourg and a renowned legal expert, Laban was a rich man. Furthermore, he had been offered a post at the University of Heidelberg at the very time at which the silent partner had requested information concerning a house or apartment in Heidelberg.

"Are there any heirs?"

"He didn't have any children. I haven't found out what became of his sister's son and daughter, but I will."

The bank closed at four. At five the employees left. At six the manager left, too. I followed her to the streetcar. It was empty and the two of us sat alone—she in the second row, and I behind her in the seventh. After a few stops she got up, and on her way out she stopped next to me and said, "You might as well come along."

20

Like those men of ours

We walked in the rain through a residential area with old villas. Some of the houses had been restored to their former splendor. Plaques bore the names of the companies, law firms, and tax consultants that now occupied them. But in other villas the stucco was crumbling, the brickwork was exposed, windows and doors were rotting, and here and there a balcony or two were missing. Frau Soboda walked in silence, and I walked in silence beside her. I followed her into one of the shabby houses. The third floor had been divided into apartments. Frau Soboda unlocked the door to one and showed me into her living room.

"It's still warm," she said, pointing to a large green tiled stove. "The fire's just died down a bit. But it'll be warmer in here in a minute." She put in some more coals and closed the fire hatch.

"I'm—"

"I know, you're with the police."

"How—"

"You look just like those men of ours used to. I mean the men from the Firm. The Stasi. The way you came into the bank and looked around. The way you didn't let the bank out of your sight all day. So one wouldn't notice right away, but if one did it didn't matter, as the game was up, anyway." She eyed me. "You are from the West, and are older than those men of ours used to be. And yet . . ."

We were still standing. "May I hang up my coat outside? I don't want to get your rug wet."

She laughed. "Give it to me. That's something those former men of ours wouldn't have asked." When she returned she offered me a chair, and when we were seated she said: "But I'm glad it's all over."

I waited, but she was lost in thought. "Would you like to start from the beginning?" I asked.

She nodded. "I didn't notice anything for a long time. I think that's why they let me run the bank. I learned my trade in the old East German days. I had no idea about the way banking is done in the West, and had to work my way into it slowly, and with difficulty." She patted down the cover on the little table that stood between her chair and mine. "I really thought this was the chance of a lifetime. Many of the other East German savings banks were shut down and many of my colleagues were let go, and those who were allowed to stay had to go stand at the back of the line. As for me, I went from being bank teller to bank manager. For a while I was worried that the only reason was that they wanted an old employee of the bank to fire everyone else, so that none of you guys would have to get your fingers dirty. I need not tell you that this was how things were done more often than not. And yet nobody at our Sorbian bank got fired. So I had pulled the winning ticket, and I worked my fingers to the bone, until . . . until . . . my marriage fell apart." She shook her head. "Not that it was much of a marriage. It would have fallen apart anyway. But perhaps it wouldn't have happened a year ago, when I was studying and reading like a maniac, when I could see that I was making it, that everything I'd read was coming together, everything I'd learned, seen, and done right. Even though it was mostly out of sheer luck. Now I'm sure I could easily run any bank of similar size in West Germany." She looked at me with pride. "But I wouldn't be given such a bank, especially not now."

"If I had a bank, you'd be its manager," I told her, to apologize for having thought when I first saw her that she looked like a tractor driver.

"But you don't." She smiled. While she was talking I noticed the cleverness in her tough face. Now I also saw a touch of charm.

"When did you notice what was going on?"

"About six months ago. At first I noticed only that something was wrong. It took me a while to realize what it was. I'd have been glad to go straight to the police, but the lawyer I cautiously consulted wasn't sure if I was actually allowed to go to the authorities. By all accounts, industrial law provides for the firing of a whistle-blower, even if an employer has done something he ought not to have done and the employee was right to blow the whistle. It wasn't only losing my job that I was frightened of. You see"—her eyes challenged me—"I have a knack for landing on my feet. But what about my colleagues at the bank? There are many of us, perhaps too many, and I don't think the bank will stay above water if everything comes to light."

The longer she talked the more I liked her. In the old days, I used to think that men were the realists and women the romantics. Nowadays I know it's the other way around, and that pragmatic men and romantic women were just pretending, to themselves and to others. I also know that a pragmatic woman with a heart, and a romantic man with common sense, is a rare and wonderful thing. Vera Soboda was just such a woman.

"How did you find all this out?"

"Quite by chance, the way one does. It's not as if one expects this sort of thing, or keeps an eye out for it. One of our customers insisted that she had deposited fifty marks a week earlier, on a day when she forgot to bring her savings book with her. Now she had brought her savings book in order to have her fifty-mark deposit entered, but our bank system had no record of it."

"What did you do?"

"I've known Frau Sellmann forever. She's an old lady who I'm sure scrimps and saves all she can, and she is conscientious to a fault. She had her deposit slip with her, and though it's not impossible to forge one, Frau Sellmann is no forger. So I entered the fifty marks in her savings book, and then in the evening I initiated a search through our system to see where her deposit might have ended up. Tanya, the teller who had signed the receipt, is just as conscientious as Frau Sellmann. I just cannot imagine her forgetting to deposit the money."

"Did you find the fifty marks?"

"We have a system we use and a program that tracks every step of every transaction. But we can't access it because it's there to monitor us, and the whole idea is that we shouldn't be able to manipulate it. But I'm very good with computers, so I tried to get into the program."

"And did you?"

She laughed. "You're on pins and needles."

I nodded. My fever was getting worse, and I had the feeling I couldn't hold out much longer—just a little more, and during this time I'd have to find out all I could.

"I got into the tracking program, and in fact it had registered the deposit of those fifty marks. But at the same time there was a deposit of thirty-five thousand marks to her account, more than Frau Sellmann with all her scrimping could have ever scraped together. The tracking program had recorded that the thirty-five thousand marks had not gone into Frau Sellmann's real account but into a false account that had been set up under her name. As both payments had taken place at the same time, both the fifty marks and the thirty-five thousand marks had somehow gotten into her false account. When I looked further, I found that Frau Sellmann's false account had a balance of one hundred twenty thousand marks, a good hundred thousand more than in her real account. I also found all the other accounts in which my poor Sorbian compatriots were made out to be wealthy men and women, not to mention the accounts that show poor, dead Sorbians to be alive and wealthy."

"The whole thing's quite straightforward," I said, hoping she would agree with me and elaborate further so that I might finally get some insight into all of this.

"When you own a bank," she said, "it isn't all that difficult to launder money—in this way, and I imagine in other ways, too. Once the money is in the bank, all the bank has to do is invest it in a manner so that it gets lost. They've invested most of it in Russia."

"In their own enterprises."

"I believe so." She looked at me. "What's the next step? What will the upshot be when you arrest Welker and Samarin? What will happen to the Sorbian bank?"

"I don't know. In the old days I could have called and asked Nägelsbach, but he's retired, and I'd be happy to transfer my money from the Badische Beamtenbank to the Sorbian Cooperative Bank, but it won't be enough. It wouldn't matter that I'm not part of the cooperative, would it? I'm also not an official. Schuler was a retired official, but he's dead. Can you understand that? I still don't understand why he's dead."

She looked at me in alarm.

I got up. "I've got to go. I don't want to leave still owing you an explanation, but I've got to get to bed. I'm sick. I'm running a temperature. Some skinheads threw me into the Landwehr Canal yesterday, which in a way served me right, and today I stood outdoors all day in the rain and cold. The only reason my nose isn't running is because I got some medicine, but now my head's so heavy and numb that I'd rather not have a head at all. Not to mention that I feel cold."

My teeth were chattering.

She got up. "Herr . . ."

"Self."

"Herr Self, shall I call you a cab?"

"It would be best if I could lie down on your sofa and you'd lie down with me till I warmed up again."

She didn't lie down with me. But she set me up on her sofa, heaped all the comforters and woolen blankets she could find over me, gave me two aspirin, made me some grog, and placed her cool hand on my hot forehead till I fell asleep.

21

Childish faces

When I woke up it was bright daylight. My suit was draped neatly over a chair and there was a note on the table: "I'll try to be back by four. Hope you feel better." I made some tea in the kitchen, took the cup to the sofa, and lay down again.

I had regained all my senses. But my nose was runny, my throat was sore, and I felt so weak that I wanted nothing more than to doze all day and drowsily look out the window, watching the wind drive the gray clouds across the blue sky and rustle through the bare twigs of the plane tree. I wanted to listen to the rain and watch the raindrops running down the windowpanes. Not think about Schuler, whom I could have saved if I had not been too slow; not about the skinheads

I'd let make a fool of me; and not about Karl-Heinz Ulbrich, whom I found touching even though I didn't like him. But whenever I dozed off, it all came back: Ulbrich seeking my paternal acknowledgement and backing, the skinheads and my fear, Schuler staggering toward me with his attaché case. So I got up and sat by the tiled stove and thought about everything that Vera Soboda had told me. She was right; when you own a bank it's not hard to launder money. The dirty money went into the false accounts of customers at the Sorbian Cooperative Bank, accounts that were run in a secret parallel system, and from there the money would be invested in companies that only showed losses and perhaps didn't even exist. That way the customers were rid of money they didn't even know they had, while the owners of the dirty money and the companies ended up with clean money. Frau Sellmann had a hundred thousand marks too much in her account; even if the idea wasn't to deposit an extra hundred thousand marks in every illegitimate account, but simply three or four times the amount that people had in their legitimate accounts, with a few thousand clients, millions upon millions of marks could be laundered.

Schuler must have found out where dirty money was being kept. Why hadn't he gone to the police? Why had he come to me? Because he didn't want to destroy Welker, his former pupil and the son of his friend and patron?

It was noon. I looked around the apartment. The kitchen area had once been part of the bathroom, and the living room was also her bedroom, the sofa her bed, and she had spent the night in the covered veranda. She also had an office with a desk, a computer, and a hammock. As the manager of a bank she ought to be able to afford more. What did she do with her money? Next to the desk were photographs of her with and without her husband, with and without a child, a girl with a high forehead and blond hair, as dainty as Frau Soboda was robust. Might the girl not be a daughter but a niece? I took a sheet of paper from her desk.

Dear Frau Soboda,

Thank you for everything you have done for me. I enjoyed staying at your place, even though I admit I am somewhat shaken that I might look like a man from the Stasi. I slept a long time, my temperature is almost gone, and I'm glad that my head is back on my shoulders.

I'm not a policeman. I am a private investigator and, though it may be hard for you to believe, Herr Welker hired me: I am investigating a matter for him that I am quite certain is merely a pretext. But I do not know for what.

I wish I knew what it was. I also hope to know more before I go to the police with what I know. I'll inform you when I get to that point.

Best regards,
Gerhard Self

I added my address and phone number. Then I called a taxi and headed for the train station. By late afternoon I was back in Berlin.

I don't know what devil possessed me. Instead of rebooking my flight and leaving immediately or discarding the ticket and taking the next train home, I settled in again at the hotel on Unter den Linden, went strolling through Berlin again, and ended up once more at the Hallesches Tor metro station. What was I looking for? I had also gone to the street where I grew up. The hydrant where I pumped some water with a large lever, just for fun, might well have been the same one where I had pumped water as a child. I wasn't quite sure.

It was the others who were at the Hallesches Tor this time. Black pants and jackets, and a few girls in grungy black outfits. I didn't recognize them, but they recognized me. "That's the old guy who was shouting 'Heil Hitler' the other day. You're an old Nazi, right?"

I didn't say anything. Hadn't they seen that I'd been forced to play along, and that I'd ended up in the canal?

They crowded around me, forcing me back against the railing. What childish faces, I thought. What foolish, eager, childish faces. But I felt I had been punished sufficiently two days ago for the "Heil Hitlers." Perhaps I merited more punishment for the many "Heil Hitlers" all those years ago and all the misery I had caused as public prosecutor. But not from these children.

"Please let me through."

"We're the Antifa!" They, too, had a leader of the pack, a tall thin fellow wearing glasses. When I tried to wriggle my way through, he pushed his hand against my chest. "We don't want any fascists in our city."

"Aren't there enough young people you can teach that lesson to?"

"One thing at a time! First the older generation, then the young!" He was still pressing his hand against my chest.

I lost control of myself. I hit his hand away and gave his foolish face two slaps—one on the left cheek and one on the right. He threw himself at me and pressed me against the railing. This time there was no "One, two, three!"—the others helped him silently with set mouths until I hung head-down. I fell with a splash into the water.

I was standing once again on the sidewalk, taxis kept driving by, first slowing down when the driver saw me wave, then speeding away when the driver saw my wet clothes. A patrol car did the same. Finally a young woman had mercy on me, asked me into her car, and dropped me off in front of my hotel. The doorman who'd been on duty two days before was standing at his post again. He recognized me and laughed out loud. I didn't think it was funny.

22

An old circus horse

I didn't find saying good-bye to Berlin at all difficult. I looked down as the plane flew in a wide arc over the city on Saturday morning. A lot of water, a lot of green, straight and crooked streets, large and small houses, churches with towers, churches with cupolas—everything a city needs. One can't deny that Berlin is a big city. That Berliners are unfriendly, their children unruly, their taxi drivers inhospitable, their policemen incompetent, and their doormen impolite—perhaps that is to be expected in a city that has been subsidized for decades. But I don't like it.

I arrived in Mannheim feeling just as grim, chilled, and feverish as I had felt leaving Berlin. Nägelsbach had left a message on my machine that my car had been moved from outside the police station, where I had left it, to the Werderstrasse. He had seen to it that it wouldn't be towed to the Friesenheimer Insel outside of town but parked near my place, and I wouldn't have to pay a fine. Georg was back from Strasbourg and wanted to report to me. Brigitte had taken Manu to Beerfelden for the weekend. Welker was urging me to meet with him, by Sunday morning at the latest: he'd be in his office over the weekend and would be expecting my call and visit. Among the messages there was also a whining one from Karl-Heinz Ulbrich: This isn't right, we need to talk. He'd gotten himself a cell phone and wanted me to call him. I erased his message without taking down the number.

The few steps from my office to my apartment were like wading through mud, and on the stairs I worried that again I wouldn't make it, like before Christmas. I got into bed and called Philipp. He wasn't on duty at the hospital and came over right away.

"I can't tell you how relieved I am you're here," I told him. "Will you give me a quick checkup and get me a prescription? I have to be back on my feet by tomorrow."

He took out his stethoscope. "Let's see if this thing still works—I haven't used it since I was an intern."

I coughed, held my breath, breathed in and out. There was a rattling; I could hear it, too. His face looked grave, and he got up. "You're going to have to take some antibiotics. I'll go down to the drugstore and get some for you. As for your being up and about tomorrow, forget it."

"I've got to get up."

"When I get back you can explain why, and I'll talk you out of it."

He took my key and left. Or was he still standing at my bedside? No, he was back already with the medicine and had brought a glass of water from the kitchen.

"Take this."

I'd fallen asleep.

He got a chair from the kitchen and sat down next to my bed. "It's just a matter of time before you have your next heart attack, even though you smoke less. If you're in a weakened condition, like you are now, and also exert yourself, the risks are especially high. I know you'll do what you want, but the question is simple enough: Is whatever you're intending to do tomorrow worth the risk? Aren't there things that are worth more? More important cases, an adventure with Manu, a wild night with Brigitte?"

"There was a time when you'd have put a wild night with Brigitte at the top of the list, or you'd have prescribed me two rambunctious nurses," I said.

He grinned. "When I think of all the suggestions I made! Just pearls before swine! You should thank your lucky stars that you've got Brigitte. Without her you'd be a sour old grouch."

"What about you?"

"Me? I'm glad I've got my little Furball. I think I'll brace myself and give marrying her another go."

I thought of the first time he'd given marrying Füruzan a "go." I had waited for Philipp with Füruzan—a proud, beautiful Turkish nurse—her mother, and her brother. Then, right at the door of the town hall, Philipp, dead drunk, had announced that he couldn't go through with the marriage, and Füruzan's brother had attacked him with a knife. I thought how Philipp had lain in the hospital recuperating from his wounds and had gone off women.

"And you'll never touch another woman?" I asked him now.

He raised his hands and slowly lowered them again. "When a woman looks at me, I look back. I'm like an old circus horse. When he hears all the commotion and fanfare, he goes trotting around the arena. But he'd much rather be in his stable, munching oats. And just as the public can tell that the circus horse is old, even though he goes trotting around the arena, women notice it in me, too, even though I look at them and flirt and know what they like to hear and how they like to be touched." He stared into the distance.

"Did you see it coming?" I asked.

"I always thought that when the time comes all my memories would compensate me for what the present would be depriving me of. But remembering doesn't work. I can tell myself what was, and how it was, and that it was great; I can conjure up pictures in my inner eye. But I can't conjure up the feeling. I know that a woman's breasts felt really good, or her bottom, or that she had a certain way of moving when she was on top of me that was just . . . or that she would . . . But I only know it, I don't experience it. I don't feel the feeling."

"Well, that's the way of the world. Memories are memories."

"No!" he countered vehemently. "When I remember how furious I was when they remodeled our operating theater, I'm furious all over again. When I remember what pleasure I had when I bought my boat, I relive that pleasure. Only love eludes memory." He got up. "You have to get some sleep. Don't do anything foolish tomorrow."

I lay there staring into the twilight. Did love elude memory? Or was it desire? Was my friend mixing up love and desire?

I decided I was not going to call Welker the following day. As it was, I hadn't decided what to tell him or what to threaten him with or how to stop him. I would sleep and get some rest. I would give Turbo the can of mackerel I had brought him from Cottbus. I would read a book and play a game of chess with Keres or Euwe or Bobby Fisher. I would cook. I would drink red wine. Philipp hadn't said anything about my antibiotic clashing with red wine or red wine clashing with my antibiotic. I'd postpone my heart attack to some other time.

23

Cat and mouse

But at nine o'clock I was awakened by a call from Welker.

"Where did you get my number?" My number has been unlisted for five years.

"I know it's Sunday morning, but I must insist that you drop by my office. You can park inside the gate, that way it'll be . . ." He broke off. I already knew the game well enough: Welker would start talking, the receiver would then be covered, and suddenly Samarin would be on the line. "We'll be expecting you around noon. Twelve o'clock."

"How do I get inside the gate?"

He hesitated. "Ring three times."

So that was that as far as catching up on my sleep was

concerned, or getting some rest, cooking, reading, or playing chess. I filled the tub, sprinkled some rosemary into the water, and got in. Turbo appeared, and I irritated him with a few well-aimed drops. Some water on the thumb, flicked off with the index finger: with a little training you can become quite a champion. And I have many years of training behind me.

Why did I hesitate about how to handle my client's money laundering? I didn't really have much of a choice. The TV channels might not be interested in the Russian Mafia—which has no class, no style, no tradition, no religion, and presumably no sense of humor—but the police most certainly would be, which was only right. Why didn't I give them a call? Why hadn't I called them yesterday? I realized that I just couldn't bring myself to do that as long as Welker was still my client.

So the early call and the appointment at noon did have a good side: I could close my case. I brought the phone to the bathtub and called Georg, who told me the rest of the sad tale of the Laban family. Laban's niece died of tuberculosis in the 1930s in Davos, and his nephew had killed himself and his wife during the Nazi rampages of the Kristallnacht. The nephew's son and his wife had died childless in London, while his daughter had not managed to flee abroad in time. She had gone into hiding when the deportations to the concentration camps began and was never heard from again. There was nobody who could claim the inheritance.

I got out of the tub and dried myself. If you ask me, Dorian Gray exaggerated. As one grows older one needn't want to look twenty year after year, and it was no surprise that he didn't come to a good end. But why can't I look sixty-six? By what right did my arms and legs become so thin? What right did their former mass have to leave its old home and find a new one under my belly button? Couldn't my flesh have consulted me before going off and resettling someplace else?

I stopped grumbling and pulled in my stomach when I put on the corduroys I hadn't worn in ages, a turtleneck, and a leather jacket, and before you knew it I could almost pass for sixty-six. Over breakfast I put on an old Udo Jürgens record. At quarter past twelve I was in Schwetzingen.

Samarin took me to the apartment in the upper story, and as we walked through the old banking hall and the new office area, he and I played cat and mouse.

"I hear you were at the Mannheim police station," he said.

"I took your advice."

"My advice?"

"Your advice not to keep what isn't mine. I gave it to the police. That way whoever it belongs to can go get it."

Welker was on edge. He barely listened to my report concerning the silent partner. He looked at his watch again and again, his head cocked as if he were waiting for something. When I finished my report, I expected some questions—if not about the silent partner, then at least about Schuler, the black attaché case, my going to the police, or my disappearance from Mannheim. Questions that were so pressing that they had to be answered on a Sunday morning. But no questions came. Welker sat there as if more important issues were at hand, issues he could barely wait to come up. But he didn't say anything. He got up. I got up, too.

"So that's that," I said. "I'll be sending you my bill."

And yet this former client of mine might well be in jail by tomorrow morning and not get to see my bill for some years to come. Six? Eight? What does one get for organized crime?

"I'll walk you to your car," Samarin said.

Samarin walked ahead, I followed, and Welker walked behind me as we made our way through the offices and down the stairs. I took leave of the old counters with their wooden bars, the inlaid panels, and the benches with the green velvet cushions. It was a pity; I would have liked to sit on one of these benches for a while and muse over the currents and vicissitudes of life. By the gate I said good-bye to Welker. He was in a curious nervous state, his hands cold and sweaty, his face flushed, and his voice shaking. Did he suspect what I was going to do? But how could he?

Samarin did not respond to my good-bye. He pressed the lower of the two buttons near the gate and it swung open. I went to my car, got in, and fastened my seat belt. I glanced behind me. Welker's face was so tense, so desperate, that I was taken aback, while Samarin looked burly and grim, but at the same time pleased. I was glad to get away.

I started the car and drove off.

PART TWO

I

Drive!

I drove off, and at the same moment Welker leapt toward me.
I saw his face, his gaping mouth and wide eyes, at the
passenger-side window and heard his fists banging against
the car door. What does he want? I thought. I stepped on the
brake, leaned across the seat, and rolled down the window.
He reached in, pulled up the lock, tore the door open, jumped
into the car, slumped down on the passenger seat, reached
over me, locked my door, did the same with his, and rolled his
window back up, all the while shouting: "Drive! Drive, damn
it! As fast as you can!"

   I didn't react immediately, but then I saw the yard gate
beginning to swing shut, threw the gear into reverse, and made

it out just in time, with only a few scratches to the front fenders. Samarin was running alongside the car, trying to get the door open. "Faster!" Welker kept shouting, holding on to the door from inside. "Faster!"

I floored the gas pedal and raced over the Schlossplatz into the Schlosstrasse. "Quick, give me your cell phone!" Welker said, reaching over to me.

"I don't have one."

"Damn!" He slammed his fists down on the dashboard. "How can you not have a cell phone?"

I pulled into a parking lot in the Hebelstrasse and stopped in front of a public phone where he could use my phone card. "Not here! Let's go where there are lots of people!"

It was Sunday noon and the parking lot was still empty. But what was he afraid of? That Samarin and a few young men in suits would turn up and abduct him? I drove to the Schwetzingen train station, which wasn't exactly pulsating with life, but there were taxis, a waiting bus, a newsstand, an open ticket counter, and some passengers. Welker took my phone card, his eyes darting in all directions, and went to a phone. I saw him pick up the receiver, insert the card, dial a number, wait, and begin to talk. Then he hung up and leaned against the wall. He looked as if he would collapse if the wall weren't there.

I waited. Then I got out and walked over to him. He was crying. Crying silently, tears running down his cheeks, gathering on his chin, and dripping onto his sweater. He didn't wipe them away. His arms hung limply at his sides, as if bereft of all power. He suddenly noticed that I was standing in front of him. "They've got my children. They drove off with them half an hour ago."

"Drove off? Where to?"

"Zurich, back to their boarding school. But they'll reach the boarding school only if I go back to Samarin." He straightened up and wiped away his tears.

"Please tell me what's going on. What are you mixed up in? What is this all about?"

"As a private investigator, are you pledged to silence? Like a doctor or priest?" But he didn't wait for an answer. He began to talk and talk. It was a cold day, and after a while my legs and stomach began to hurt from standing. But his flow of words didn't stop, and I didn't interrupt him. A woman wanted to use the phone, so we got back into the car. I started the engine and put the heater on high, whatever the damage to the environment. He ended up weeping again.

2

Double insurance

His story began in August 1991. There had been a failed military putsch in Moscow. Gorbachev's star was on the wane, Yeltsin's on the rise. Gregor Samarin had proposed that Weller & Welker send him to Russia to look into investment opportunities; the failed putsch signified that the fate of Communism was sealed and that the triumph of capitalism was unstoppable. This was the perfect moment, he argued, to make investments in Russian enterprises, and with his knowledge of Russia, its language, and its people, he could guarantee Weller & Welker a competitive edge.

Until then Samarin had been a jack-of-all-trades at the bank: chauffeur and errand boy, a handyman at the bank and the apartment, someone who could help out as a teller and with the bookkeeping and filing. He had completed high school but had not been interested in continuing with his studies—nor did anybody encourage him to. Even as a schoolboy he had made himself useful, and it was quite convenient that he was even more available now. He lived in the servant's room in old Herr Welker's house in the Gustav-Kirchhoff-Strasse and was paid a modest salary and given a little extra whenever he wanted to buy something or go on vacation. But he rarely asked for anything. He had studied Russian at school because of his mother, and he traveled to Russia once a year. He drove cars handed down to him by the two families. He had become a fixture.

Everyone was taken aback by his idea about Russia. But then again, why shouldn't he be given a chance to prove himself? If nothing came of it, he would at least have gotten out and about and had a vacation of sorts. If something did come of it—which nobody really believed would happen—then so much the better. It was decided that he would be sent to Russia.

Samarin stayed there for almost six months. He kept in touch with regular phone calls, faxes, and telegrams. He proposed a series of investments in the energy sector, from electrical power plants in Moscow and Sverdlovsk to securing drilling options in Kamchatka. From time to time he introduced Russian businessmen who were looking to invest money in the West, who would then turn up in Schwetzingen. None of his schemes panned out, nor did the Russian businessmen. But Gregor Samarin returned to Germany a changed man. Not only did he bring back a Russian accent, he also dressed and comported himself as if he were one of the bank's directors. Old Herr Weller had just retired and moved to the assisted-living section of the Augustinum. Bertram and Stephanie didn't want to hurt Gregor. Hadn't they resolved to be different as directors than their fathers had been and to avoid all arrogance and conceit? Hadn't Bertram and Gregor grown up together? Hadn't Gregor always been fully committed to the families and their bank?

Then Gregor began talking about Weller & Welker initiating a takeover of the Sorbian Cooperative Bank, and Bertram and Stephanie tried to make him see why a takeover would be a mistake. The future of Weller & Welker lay in investment counseling, not in handling small savings accounts. The bank had survived the crisis of the eighties by downsizing, dropping everything that was inessential, and concentrating exclusively on what was essential. But Gregor Samarin wouldn't let go. One day he came back from a trip to Berlin and announced that he had completed negotiations he'd been involved in for weeks with the Treuhand Agency, which was privatizing former East German state institutions such as the bank, and that he had bought the bank for a song. He had forged a power of attorney, and they could report him, take him to court, and have him thrown in prison if they liked; if they took action fast enough they could perhaps even cancel the deal with the Treuhand Agency. But how would that look for Weller & Welker? How thrilled would their clients be, reading about all the turmoil in the firm? Wouldn't it make more sense to let him handle the Sorbian Cooperative Bank? He'd get it back on its feet. It was the bank of the common man, and he knew all about the common man since he was one himself. Didn't Weller & Welker owe him the chance?

Bertram and Stephanie gave in, and to their surprise it

seemed to work. After a year, the Sorbian bank might not have been showing a profit, but it wasn't showing a loss, either—and this despite the extensive modernization of its main branch in Cottbus and the branches in the provinces, and despite all the Sorbian Cooperative employees having been kept on, as the Treuhand Agency had been promised as part of the takeover. It seemed that the East Germans had more money than was generally assumed. Gregor Samarin also seemed to have the knack of procuring subsidies from local, state, and European institutions. An East German success story!

Until Stephanie caught on. She didn't trust the pretty picture, didn't trust Gregor, and had no scruples about peeking into Gregor's filing cabinet or his computer. An émigré Russian economist whom she hired in Berlin helped her figure out what she didn't understand. She told Bertram what she found out, and together they confronted Gregor. They gave him a month to remove himself and his dirty deals from their bank and their lives. They would not go to the police, but they didn't want anything to do with him.

Gregor's reaction was quite unexpected. He had no idea what had gotten into them. He had done them no wrong, he had even furthered their business, and now they wanted to ruin him. He was a businessman—he had obligations and could not afford not to fulfill them. He was going to stay right where he was! And while they were at it, he was sick and tired of having to transport the money from the West to Cottbus. Henceforth, he'd collect the money and feed it into the system right here in Schwetzingen.

"We're giving you one month to remove yourself," Stephanie said, "and that's that. Don't force us to go to the police."

Two weeks later Stephanie was dead. If Bertram wasn't prepared to play Samarin's game, his children would be next—first one, and then the other—and in the end it would be his turn. Samarin wasn't about to give up all he'd worked for.

The children were then sent to school in Switzerland, with two young men in dark suits or in ski suits, in tennis or jogging outfits, or in hiking gear—always at their sides. Bertram had been forced to explain to the headmaster that the men were bodyguards; after the mysterious disappearance of their mother—involving a possible case of abduction or blackmail—one couldn't be too careful. The headmaster had no objections. The young men kept a certain discreet distance, to the extent they could.

"As for me," Welker continued, "you yourself have seen what I've been reduced to. I had to move from my house to the bank, and I haven't been allowed to take a single step on my own. Then you showed up, and I managed to draw you into all this with the tale of the silent partner. In Gregor's view, your investigation would hardly pose a threat; not to mention that he was worried that you'd grow suspicious if he threw you out. I didn't hire you because of this idiotic silent partner. I was hoping all along that you'd realize what was going on at my bank and that you'd be at hand when the time came. But you weren't."

I looked at him blankly.

"No, no, I'm not reproaching you; far from it. I'd only hoped you might notice what was going on. I'd hoped it might be a sign to you that something wasn't right at the bank when Gregor wouldn't let me call you, when he didn't give a damn about what I said, or that time when he exploded and ordered me to believe what he says, or when the attaché case was so important to him while I didn't show any interest in it. I'd also hoped you'd come earlier today. But I'd hoped, too, that the children would stay longer. I wanted to get out of Gregor's grip with your help while the children were visiting some friends of mine in Zurich. Do you see what he's done? He has gotten himself double insurance: if the children elude his grip he still has me, and if I elude his grip—for instance, at a business meeting or social occasion, where he cannot intervene in what I say—then he's got the children. While they were at my friends' place in Zurich, he lost them. Now he's got them again."

"We should go to the police."

"Are you out of your mind? They've got my kids. They'll kill them if I go to the police." He stared at his hands. "The only place I can go is back to the bank. That's the only place I can go." This time he cried like a child, sobbing pitifully, his shoulders shaking.

3

No longer my kind of world

I assured Welker that there was no reason he couldn't wait a few hours before going back. Nothing would happen to the children as long as Samarin couldn't get in touch with him. The children would be of no use to Samarin if they were dead; he needed them in order to threaten Welker. And he could only do that if he managed to talk to Welker.

"How is waiting going to do any good?"

"A few hours without Gregor Samarin—isn't that something? I'd like to have a word with an old friend of mine, a retired police officer. I know you don't want to hear of the police being involved. But things can't go on this way, neither for the children nor for you. Something has to give. And we can do with all the help we can get."

"Well, go ahead."

I called Nägelsbach and then Philipp. I asked Philipp if we could use his apartment as a meeting place, since Gregor's men knew where I lived and probably had already followed me to Nägelsbach's and Brigitte's. Avoiding the autobahn, we meandered over Plankstadt, Grenzhof, Friedrichsfeld, and Rheinau to Philipp's apartment at the Waldparkdamm. There was no blue Mercedes anywhere to be seen, nor a black or green one, and there were no young men in dark suits. On the Stephanienufer promenade along the Rhine, couples who had already had lunch were pushing baby strollers while barges chugged along the river.

Welker was wary. Nägelsbach brought his wife, and Philipp insisted, if we were going to get together at his place, on being present and listening in. Welker looked from one of us to another and then glanced at Philipp's bedroom door, which stood ajar, revealing the mirror on the ceiling above the water bed. He turned to me and said, "Are you sure that . . ."

I nodded and began to tell his story. From time to time he added something, finally taking over himself. In the end, he began to cry again. Frau Nägelsbach got up, sat on the armrest of his chair, and hugged him.

"No longer my kind of world," Nägelsbach said, shaking his head sadly. "Not that everything in my world was right— I wouldn't have become a policeman if it had been. But money was money, a bank was a bank, and a crime was a crime. Murder was driven by passion, jealousy, or desperation, and if it was driven by greed, it was burning greed.

Calculated murder, laundering millions, a bank that's a madhouse in which the insane have locked up the doctors and nurses—all that is foreign to me."

"Oh, that's enough," Frau Nägelsbach said irritably. "You've been talking like this for weeks now. Can't you forget being grouchy about your retirement and come to grips with it and tell this poor fellow and your friends something that might be useful to them? You were a good policeman. I was always proud of you and want to continue being proud."

Philipp stepped in. "I understand him. It's no longer my kind of world, either. I'm not quite sure why: the end of the Cold War, capitalism, globalization, the Internet? Or is it that people no longer have morals?" I must have been staring at him nonplussed. He stared back coolly. "You seem to think that morality isn't my thing? The fact that I have loved many women doesn't mean I don't have any morals. Let's not forget that wherever money's being laundered, women are being exploited, too. No, I'm not prepared to give up my world without a fight, and I hope the rest of you aren't, either."

Somewhat taken aback, I looked at Philipp, and then at Nägelsbach.

"Without a fight?" Frau Nägelsbach said, shaking her head. "You don't have to prove to the world that you're not yet ready for the scrapheap or that you can still show the younger generation a thing or two. Call the police! See to it that they don't rattle Samarin! You know the right people, Rudi. If Samarin catches on that the game is up, he won't be stupid enough to harm the children."

"I don't think he'd do anything to them, either. But as for being sure—no, I'm not sure. Are you? A culprit might see reason when the game's up, but he might also lose his reason. So far I haven't seen Samarin lose his cool. But recently he almost did, and I'm afraid that if he does in fact explode he'd be capable of anything," I said.

"Of one thing you can be certain," Welker cut in. "He's quite capable of exploding. He's quite capable of murder, too. No, going to the police is not an option. Thank you very much, but I—" Welker stood up.

"Sit down, please," I said. "We must use what we have: a doctor, an ambulance."

Philipp nodded.

"A policeman in uniform."

Nägelsbach laughed. "If I still can squeeze into my uniform—I haven't worn it in years."

"We also have the choice of the meeting place. Herr Welker, you need to give a convincing performance over the phone—you must sound so panic-stricken that Samarin will be ready to meet with you wherever you want rather than having you flip out completely. Can you manage that?"

Philipp grinned. "Don't worry. I can get Herr Welker there."

"We'll tell Samarin to come to the Mannheim Water Tower," Nägelsbach said, sliding an ashtray to the center of the table to represent the water tower. He put a newspaper in front of it to represent the Kaiserring and pointed at it with his pen. "Needless to say, Samarin will position his men around the water tower. If he has four cars, he'll have them wait by the four streets leading away from the tower. But he can't have all his men waiting in the cars, and if he . . . ."

Nägelsbach explained his plan, answered questions, and weighed objections, and the venture took shape. Frau

Nägelsbach looked at him with pride. I, too, was proud of my friends. I was particularly amazed at Philipp's calm concentration and authority. Did he plan his surgical operations this way? Did he prepare his colleagues for their roles on the surgical team the way he was preparing Welker for his role on the phone? He talked at him, cross-examined him, ridiculed him, reassured him, and yelled at him, and soon enough he had shaken him so thoroughly that when Welker called Samarin he was on the verge of losing it.

Samarin agreed to the meeting: five o'clock at the water tower. "No police. You and I will talk. You will speak to your children on the cell phone, and then we'll drive back to Schwetzingen."

4

Blow-by-blow

If wishes came true, I would be living in one of the pavilions on top of the two elegant sandstone houses at the corner of Friedrichsplatz and Augustaanlage. I would put a lounger out on the balcony, set up the Zeiss telescope I inherited from my father, and watch what happened from a distance. Instead, I found myself standing by the water tower, where I couldn't be of any use.

Welker got there well before five. He walked around the water tower, looked into the empty basins, and kept peering from the Rosengarten all the way to the Kunsthalle Museum. He was very nervous. He kept hugging his chest as if he were trying to hold on to himself. He walked too fast, and whenever he stopped he stepped nervously from one foot to the other. Nägelsbach, in his police uniform, sat on a bench, relaxed as if enjoying a break. His wife was sitting next to him.

From the pavilion I would probably also have had all of Samarin's men in view. I saw the blue Mercedes—it was standing in front of the bus station on the Kaiserring, and a man was sitting at the wheel. I didn't see the other young men. I didn't see Samarin, either, until he crossed the Kaiserring and came walking toward Welker. He had a heavy, strong gait, as if nothing could sway or stop him. More likely than not, he had inspected the perimeter and had assured himself that everything was fine. If Welker had involved the police, they would not have sent a policeman in uniform to the meeting place and have him sitting next to a woman. Nor would the police have tolerated my presence. Samarin peered at the water tower, shook his head, and chuckled.

Later I forgot to ask Welker what Samarin had said, and what his reply had been. They did not talk for long. We had planned everything blow-by-blow.

The ambulance waited in the Kunststrasse until the light turned green. It drove across the Kaiserring and around the fountain in front of the water tower and turned on its siren and flashing lights a few meters away from Welker and Samarin. Samarin was annoyed. He turned and looked at the ambulance. Philipp, in a white coat, came out from the front, and Füruzan and another nurse hopped out from the back, in uniform and wheeling a stretcher. Then Samarin saw Frau Nägelsbach collapsed in front of the bench, and his annoyance subsided at the very moment Philipp placed a hand on his shoulder and plunged a syringe into his arm. Samarin staggered, and it looked as if Philipp were grabbing hold of him to steady him and prop him up. Then Samarin collapsed onto the stretcher, which in the twinkling of an eye was wheeled into the ambulance. The nurses pulled the doors shut, Philipp jumped into the driver's seat, and the ambulance sped off along the Friedrichsring. Nägelsbach saw to his wife, who was savoring her role by not regaining consciousness. She came to her senses only once the ambulance's siren died away in the distance, and Nägelsbach walked her to the taxi stand in front of the Deutsche Bank. Within a minute it was all over.

The Mercedes lunged forward with squealing tires, tore over the median strip and the streetcar tracks, and sped along the Friedrichsring in fruitless pursuit of the ambulance. I still couldn't see the other young men. None of the people strolling in the park stopped: nobody was surprised, nobody spoke to anyone, nobody asked what had happened. It had all happened so quickly.

I sat down on the bench where the Nägelsbachs had been sitting and lit one of my rare cigarettes. Rare cigarettes don't taste good. They taste like one's first cigarette, which doesn't taste good, either. In half an hour Samarin would regain consciousness in a windowless storeroom in the hospital, laced into a straitjacket and strapped to the bed. I would negotiate with him—we knew each other. Welker insisted that Samarin be exchanged for his children. He wanted Samarin to experience his defeat to the fullest. "Otherwise he'll never leave me in peace."

5

In the dark

I found Samarin with his eyes closed. There wasn't enough space for a chair; I leaned against the wall and waited. He was still in a straitjacket and strapped to the bed.

He opened his eyes, and I noticed that he'd been keeping them shut only in order to feel, hear, and sniff out my mood and state of mind. He looked at me stonily but said nothing.

"Welker wants his children back. He will exchange you for his children. And he wants you out of his life and his bank."

Samarin smiled. "So that all will be right with the world once more. Those up there among themselves, and we down here among ourselves."

I didn't say anything.

"How long do you intend to keep me here?"

I shrugged. "As long as necessary. This room isn't used. If you make trouble, you'll be pumped full of pills and dragged before a judge, who'll have you committed to a psychiatric ward. Though you should really be dragged to court for murder. But that can come later."

"If I don't return to my men soon they will harm the children. That was the plan: if something happens to me, something will happen to the children."

I shook my head. "Think about it. I'll be back in an hour."

Philipp, Füruzan, and her colleague were in the nurses' room drinking cognac. Füruzan was fluttering adoringly around Philipp. The other nurse was thrilled at having been taken along on a mission that seemed important and dangerous, even though she didn't quite understand it. Philipp had regained his debonair swagger, kept going over the escapade with glee, and was bubbling over with excitement. "His look when he felt the prick of the needle! And the way Frau Nägelsbach lay on the ground! How fast and smoothly it went! And the wild drive with sirens blaring!"

Welker relaxed only gradually. At the water tower he had sat down silently beside me on the bench. A few minutes later we got in the taxi the Nägelsbachs had sent us from the taxi stand. Before we had the driver take us to the hospital we drove through the streets of Mannheim until we were certain that nobody was following us. Throughout the trip, Welker had sat pale and silent. Now he was listening to Philipp as if he couldn't believe what had happened. "Can I have a cognac, too?"

When the hour was up, I went back to Samarin.

"What about my money?"

"Your money?"

"Okay, only part of it is mine. That's why I need it. My . . . my business partners will not be too happy if their money's gone."

"If you will disappear more reliably with the money than you would without it, I'm certain Welker won't mind your taking it. I'll ask him." I left and talked to Welker.

Welker recoiled. "Good God! The last thing I want is his dirty money! If I had found it, I'd have given it to charity. Once it's gone, it's gone: let him come tomorrow and take it."

I reported this to Samarin. He looked stunned. "That's what Welker said? The meanest and most miserly man I know?"

"That's what he said."

Samarin closed his eyes.

"You need more time? I'll come back later."

Philipp wanted to head out with the others to eat, drink, and celebrate. "We'll go now, and you can follow us later. The Nägelsbachs will be coming, too. When Samarin finally plays along, it'll still be hours before the children get here. You don't have to stand guard over him. He won't get away, and if he kicks up a fuss the night nurse will give him an injection."

"Sure, go ahead. I'll stay here and maybe catch an hour or two of sleep."

I sat in the nurses' room and heard the others' laughter along the corridor. Then the elevator doors closed, swallowing their laughter, and there was silence except for the soft hum of the central heating. We had decided to tell Samarin as late as possible the time and place of the exchange so he would have just enough time to tell his people where to go. For now he was only to instruct them to bring the children to Mannheim.

"I've got to pee," he said when I returned to his room.

"I can't untie you."

Though he was wearing the straitjacket and was strapped to the bed, he looked strong and dangerous. I went to the nurses' room and found a urine bottle. He turned his head away as I unbuttoned his pants, pulled down his underwear, took out his penis, and held it as best I could into the opening of the bottle.

"Go ahead," I said.

When I had zipped him up again he looked at me. "Thanks." After a while he asked me, "Who am I supposed to have murdered?"

"Oh, come on now. First Welker's wife, and then . . . Not that I can prove it, but I am certain that someone frightened Schuler to death. Whether it was you or your mafiosi hardly matters."

"I had known Stephanie since I was a little boy. Schuler taught me reading, writing, arithmetic, and geography. All about the Celtic Ring Wall on Heiligenberg, the Roman Bridge over the Neckar River, the Heilig-Geist Church that was torched by Mélac."

"That doesn't make the murders any better."

He waited for a while and then asked: "And what kind of connection am I supposed to have with the Mafia?"

"Stop playing games! It's hardly a secret that you've been laundering money for the Russian Mafia!"

"And that's supposed to make me and my people mafiosi?" He scoffed. "You really have no idea what's going on. Do you think Welker would still be alive if we were the Russian Mafia? Or you, for that matter? Or the bunch of clowns who've tied me up here? I was raised under the thumb of Weller and Welker and will never again allow myself to be under anyone's thumb. Yes, I launder money. And yes, I don't care who I do it for—just like any other banker. Yes, my men are Russians and professional. As for me"—he scoffed again—"I am my own boss."

He closed his eyes. Just as I thought he wouldn't say anything more he said: "I didn't like the families, neither the Wellers nor the Welkers. Bertram's grandfather and Stephanie's mother had heart. But as for Bertram's father . . . and Bertram himself . . . I ought to have killed the two of them."

"Didn't Bertram's father raise you?"

He laughed. "Siberia would have been better."

"What about Welker's kids?"

"What about them? No one's touched a hair on their heads. They think my men are their bodyguards and show off with them. The girl even flirts with them."

"Are you going to call your men? So they'll bring the kids here?"

He nodded slowly. "I'll have them set out right away. The exchange can take place tonight; I don't want to stay here like this any longer."

I found his cell phone, dialed the number he told me, and held the phone to his ear. "Speak to them in German!"

He gave them a few brief instructions. Then he asked me: "Where is the exchange to take place?"

"We'll tell you once your men are in Mannheim. By when can they make it?"

"In five hours."

"Good. We'll talk again in five hours."

I asked him if I should leave the lights on or off. He wanted to lie in the dark.

6

I guess that's that

My fever returned, and I had the night nurse give me two aspirin. "You don't look too good," she told me. "Why don't you go home and lie down?"

I shook my head. "Is there somewhere here I can sleep for a few hours?"

"We've got a second storeroom at the end of the corridor. I can have a bed set up."

As I lay there, my thoughts went to Samarin. Was the air in his room as stuffy as it was in here? Did he too feel claustrophobic? Did he hear the humming of the central heating? The room had no window, and it was pitch-dark. I held my hands in front of my face but couldn't see them.

Sometimes I think something is over and done with when in fact things are just beginning. That's what had happened to me in the morning, when Welker and Samarin had walked me to my car. Sometimes I also think I'm in the middle of something, but in fact it's already over. Was what we had wanted to bring to an end that night, in effect, already over? Of course it hadn't happened yet. But were the roles already doled out in such a way and the conditions such that whatever happened, whatever we chose to do, would still have the same result?

It was only a feeling. A fear. The fear of being too slow again, of not being fast enough to see what was actually taking place. So I weighed everything that Welker wanted, what Samarin wanted, at best what both of them would get, at worst what both would lose, what they might surprise each other with, and what they might surprise us with.

Immersed in these reflections, I fell asleep. At midnight the nurse woke me up. "The others are back."

Philipp, Nägelsbach, and Welker were sitting in the nurses' room, discussing where the exchange was to take place. Welker wanted a hidden, secret place, preferably somewhere on the outskirts of the city.

Nägelsbach preferred an open, brightly lit area, or a street somewhere downtown. "I want to be able to see these people!"

"Everybody started to chip in. So we can make sure they don't try to trick us? We'll tell them where and when we'll meet. We'll inform them of the time of our meeting so they won't be able to trick us."

"But a place that is well-lit and open . . ."

"During the exchange, one or two of us should be standing

by—someone who can see everything, but won't be seen. Someone who can step in if need be."

We decided on the Luisenpark. There were trees and shrubs behind which one could hide, but there was also a wide lawn. Samarin's men were to drive up the Werderstrasse, while we would come up the Lessingstrasse with Samarin. The exchange would take place in the middle of the park.

"Shall we do the exchange, Philipp, while the two of you stand in reserve?" I suggested. The others nodded, and Nägelsbach agreed to wear his police jacket and cap again. "Perhaps it's good if we can act as if the police are on our side."

All we could do now was wait. The big old alarm clock in the nurses' room chopped the time into little pieces. Nägelsbach had found some boxes of matches and was building a little tower, two matches one way and two the other, all the heads facing outward. Welker kept his eyes shut. His face was tense, as if he were concentrating on a difficult mathematical equation. Philipp was excitedly looking forward to the exchange as an adventure.

I went to the storeroom, turned on the light, and had Samarin talk to his men. "They've already been at the Augustaanlage for ten minutes."

"Tell them to wait there until they get further instructions."

Then I released his straps and helped him off the bed.

"What about this?" he asked, nodding down to the straitjacket that tied his arms across his chest.

I hung his coat over his shoulders. "Your men can take that off for you."

Even in the straitjacket he looked dangerous, as if he could crush me against the wall with his massive, powerful body. I kept my distance until we got to the car. He didn't say a word, not when he saw the others, among them Nägelsbach in uniform, not when Nägelsbach and I had him sit between us on the backseat, not during the drive.

We parked in the Lessingstrasse, and Welker and Nägelsbach got out and walked off. I explained to Samarin where his men were to take the children into the park, and he informed his men.

Then we got out, too, and waited at the entrance to the park, Philipp to the right of Samarin, I to the left. I couldn't see Nägelsbach and Welker, but I could see the shrubs at the other end of the park where they were going to hide. There was a half moon, bright enough for the bushes, trees, and benches to be clearly visible. The broad lawn shimmered gray. I was again beset by the fear that I had overlooked something and tried once more to weigh everything. We would send Samarin and they would send us the children. Or would they just shoot Philipp and me? Might they fail to turn up for the exchange and simply watch us and wait for us to retreat, exhausted and rattled, and then attack us? Might they . . . But my fever wouldn't let me think straight. Suddenly I found the situation unreal, bordering on the absurd. Somewhere in the distance Nägelsbach and Welker lay in wait, ready to jump out and shout "Surprise!," terrifying the enemy. Next to me Samarin stood like a bear with a ring in his nose and a chain on the ring. I wouldn't have been surprised had I heard the chain clink with every step. Philipp peered into the darkness with anxiety and pleasure, like a hunter on the prowl.

At the other end of the park headlights appeared. A big car stopped and two men got out. They opened the back doors and helped a boy and a girl get out. They walked toward us and we walked toward them. There was silence, except for our steps on the gravel.

When we were twenty meters away I said to Samarin: "Tell them to stop and send the children to us."

He barked some orders in Russian. The men stopped and said something to the boy and the girl that sounded like "Go on!" The children came toward us.

"I guess that's that," I said.

Samarin nodded and walked toward his men. He reached them and they exchanged a few words, then began to walk toward Werderstrasse. The children asked what was happening and where their father was, but Philipp growled at them to keep quiet and hurry. When we got to the entrance of the park we looked back. We looked back at the very moment it happened.

We didn't see where the shot came from; we only heard it. After the first shot there was immediately a second one. We saw Samarin collapse and his two companions crouch down to assist him, or to shield themselves, or both. I thought Oh God! and heard the silence in the park and the echo of the shots in my head, and then mayhem broke loose. Samarin's men got up and, still firing shots, ran toward their car, jumped in, and were gone.

Before I could even formulate the thought Get the children in the car, one of us with them! they were running off, shouting, "Dad!"

Welker had come out from behind the bushes at the other end of the park. He came toward them and hugged them. Philipp ran over to Samarin. When I got there, out of breath, Philipp straightened up. "He's dead."

"Where's Nägelsbach?"

Philipp looked around. "Where's Nägelsbach!" he shouted at Welker.

Welker pointed to the bushes at the end of the path. "That's where he . . ."

Then we saw him. He came toward us, dragging his feet, his hand pressed to his side.

"You idiot!" Philipp said to Welker. I had never seen him so furious. "Quick, Gerhard! We've got to get him to the car."

We ran over to Nägelsbach, propped him up, and slowly, step-by-step, made our way to the car.

Welker followed us. "What should I—"

"Wait for the police to come!"

The lights went on in some of the houses.

7

Loss of pension

We managed to get Nägelsbach to the car, to the hospital, and into the operating room. Within two hours Philipp had removed the bullet and sewn him up. He sat down next to me, took off his scrub cap and mask, and grinned at me brightly. "I've got something for you."

I took the bullet. "The police will want that," I said.

"No, this is the one the police will be wanting." He was holding another bullet between his thumb and index finger.

I looked at him nonplussed.

"He must have caught a shot years ago, and I guess it would have been too dangerous back then to remove the bullet. But the old bullet wandered and ended up not far from the new one." He looked around. "Have the police been here yet?"

I shook my head.

"It was Welker who shot Samarin, wasn't it?"

"It seems Samarin had a gun, which Welker had taken from him," I said. "Did Welker pay Samarin a visit in the storeroom?"

"Perhaps while you were asleep," Philipp said. "He didn't tell us he was going, and I didn't keep an eye out. Wouldn't Samarin have noticed Welker coming in? Wouldn't he have said something?"

"I'm sure he noticed. But as for saying something . . . No, it wouldn't have been his style to tell us that Welker had taken his gun away."

"Everything was going so well until that idiot—"

"Are you talking about me?" Welker said, suddenly appearing in front of us. "You didn't see what happened. Gregor and his men were whispering among themselves, then they reached for their weapons, and just at the moment when—"

"That's nonsense! Samarin was in a straitjacket—he could hardly have attacked anyone! And why didn't you aim at his men? Why shoot him in the back?" Philipp asked.

"I . . ." Welker fought back his tears. "I realized it wasn't going to work. Samarin had lost the battle, but not the war. I knew he'd stay on my case, and then I'd be back at square one." The tears he was fighting back were tears of anger. "Damn it, don't you see? That man was terrorizing me, month after month! He had my bank under his thumb, he murdered my wife, he threatened my children! No, I'm not sorry for what I did! I'm at my wit's end, but I'm not sorry!"

"What did the police say?"

"I didn't wait for them."

"You just up and left?"

He sat down next to us. "I found a taxi at the Collini-Center and got the children out of there. It had been a day from hell for them. I wasn't about to expose them to the ordeal of the investigation." He laid his hand on my arm. "To be honest, I wasn't sure if you were serious about the police. It's not my field—I know nothing about legal matters. Was everything we did kosher? What you and your friends did? How's the policeman, by the way?"

"He'll be back on his feet soon enough."

"Particularly in his case I was wondering what the consequences might be. Retired police officer runs amok—won't there be a disciplinary hearing? Loss of pension? I didn't want to bear that responsibility on my own, which is why I'm bringing all this up. I don't know if we can take the initiative together without consulting him. When do you think we could talk to him?"

"In a few days," Philipp said, shaking his head. "You don't seriously think we can stay out of all this. There are four of us, and then there are Füruzan, her colleague the night nurse, and Frau Nägelsbach who are in the know—not to mention that someone might have seen our car, or seen Gerhard and me with Nägelsbach when he was wounded. As for Samarin working in your bank, the police will find that out in no time at all. What will you tell them?"

"The truth. That he was involved with the Russian Mafia, that he tried to use my bank for his money-laundering schemes, that he has a number of deaths on his conscience, and that things ended up spinning out of control for him."

Philipp had called Frau Nägelsbach after operating on her husband. Now she was standing before us, eyeing us. "Who shot my husband?"

"Samarin's men."

"Why?"

"Samarin was shot."

"By whom?"

"We've just been weighing what we can and should contribute to the police investigation," Welker said, looking at Frau Nägelsbach entreatingly. "And if your husband would be pleased if the police . . . and the public . . ."

She read in his face that he was the one who had shot Samarin. She looked at him and shook her head.

"Take me to my husband," she said to Philipp. "I want to be with him when he wakes up."

They left. Welker stayed. "I'll wait for your friend. I want Nägelsbach to have whatever he needs—the best of everything, whatever the expense. You must believe me: I am terribly sorry he was shot." He looked at me as if he really were terribly sorry.

I nodded.

8

A sensitive little fellow

Outside the hospital I hoped to find a taxi at the stand. But it was still too early in the morning.

A man came up to me. At first I didn't recognize him. It was Karl-Heinz Ulbrich. "Come along, I'll drive you home."

I was too sick and too tired to turn his offer down. He took me to his car—no longer a beige Fiesta, but a light green Polo. He opened the door for me and I got in. The streets were empty, but he didn't exceed the speed limit.

"You don't look too good."

What could I say?

He laughed. "Not that I'm surprised, after all you've been through in the last twenty-four hours."

Again I said nothing.

"The water tower meeting—that was impressive. But in the park you had more luck than brains."

"You really aren't my son. You might be my deceased wife's son, but I'm not your father. When you . . . when you were conceived, I was in Poland, far away from my wife."

He wasn't swayed. "I imagine you already know that the men in the blue Mercedes are Russians. They're from Moscow, and have been in Germany for two or three years, first in Berlin, then in Frankfurt, and now here. I spoke to them in Russian, but their German isn't bad."

"They really trained you to be a pro in shadowing."

"Shadowing was always my specialty. Do you see now that we'd make a great team?"

"The two of us a team? From what I can tell, you're working not with me but against me."

He was hurt. "It's not like you're letting me work with you. Anyway, it's always good to know as much as possible."

I didn't want to hurt his feelings. "It's got nothing to do with you. It's just that I'm not a team player. I've never been one, never wanted to be one, and in my old age have no intention of becoming one." Then I felt there was no reason not to tell him the whole truth. "Not to mention that the days of small detective agencies are numbered. The only reason I've been able to stay above water is that I know everything so well here—the area, the people, their way of life—and because I know to whom I can turn for help, and when. But nowadays that's not enough. The few cases I still get barely pay for my office. If there were two of us, we wouldn't be generating any more work."

He drove along the Luisenpark. The police had gone by

now. The lawn, the bushes, and the trees were serene in the gray of dawn.

"Couldn't you . . . I don't know whether you're not my father or just don't want to be. I'd like to see a picture of my mother and find out what kind of person she was. And if you're not my father, then who might be? You must have some notion. I know you want me to leave you alone, but you can't just pretend I don't exist, that we don't exist!"

"We?"

"You don't have to keep asking the same question. You know what I'm talking about. To you we're a nuisance. You'd be happiest if we'd all stayed in the East and you would neither see us nor hear another word from us." He was hurt again. What sensitive little fellows the Stasi recruited!

"That's not true. I just got back from Cottbus and found it to be a pretty little town. I'm simply not your father. Regardless of where you're from, I'm not your father. Where are you from?"

"I'm from Prenzlau, north of Berlin."

I glanced at him sideways. His dutiful, hurt face. His neatly parted hair. His beige anorak. His shining rayon pants and light gray loafers. I'd rather have bought him something to wear than tell him about Klara. But I could see there was no way to avoid it.

"How long will you be in Mannheim? How about dropping by next Sunday? But give me a little space till then."

He nodded. "Will four o'clock do?"

We agreed on four. We pulled into the Richard-Wagner-Strasse. He got out and hurried over to my side to open the door.

"Thank you."

"I hope you feel better soon."

9

Othello

I stayed in bed all day. Turbo curled up on my legs and purred. At noon Brigitte dropped by with some chicken soup. In the evening I got a call from Philipp. His conscience was bothering him that he hadn't sent me home on Sunday. Had my heart been up to all this? Nägelsbach was doing well enough; I could visit him on Wednesday. It would be good for the three of us to talk. "The police didn't come by today. Can you imagine us staying out of the fray? I can't."

But it seemed that we *were* staying out of the fray. Welker was the only one questioned by the police. He told them about Gregor Samarin's Russian origin, his trips to Russia, the six months he spent there, his shady contacts, and his attempts to deposit large amounts of cash at Weller & Welker for supposed Russian investors. The police found the gun with which Gregor had been shot, a Malakov, in a trash can in the Luisenpark near the entrance by Werderstrasse. Samarin was found wearing a straitjacket; he had been shot in the back. An execution. People living near the park had heard shots, car doors slamming, cars driving away—a gang affair.

The Tuesday edition of the *Mannheimer Morgen* sported the headline EXECUTION IN LUISENPARK, and the Wednesday edition GANG WAR IN MANNHEIM. A few days later the papers wondered whether the Russian Mafia had taken hold in Mannheim's and Ludwigshafen's underworld. But by then it was only a small item.

Philipp and I sat by Nägelsbach's hospital bed and were strangely diffident, like boys who played a prank they have gotten away with, but for which someone else had to pay the price. The boys hadn't intended that. But it was too late to fix things. Probably Welker should be sentenced. Probably Nägelsbach and Philipp should be disciplined. Probably I should be charged with reckless something or other.

"Damn it all!" Philipp said. "In fact, I grow more optimistic every day that the police won't come looking for us. Today I'm twice as optimistic as I was on Monday, and by tomorrow I'll be four times as optimistic." He grinned.

"I'm not sure you'll see eye-to-eye with me," Nägelsbach said, looking at us apologetically, "but I don't want to keep the police out of this. I've always been on the level in matters concerning me or the law. It's true I discussed my cases with Reni, which I shouldn't have. But she's discretion personified, and I've had a case or two in my time that I couldn't have cracked without her help. But this is something else. Welker has to be charged. What Samarin did to him is no doubt an extenuating circumstance, but at the end of the day a judge must decide whether Welker is to serve a few years, end up on parole, or be acquitted."

"What does your wife think?" Philipp asked.

"Her view is . . ." He blushed. "She says it's a matter of my soul, that she and I can handle the consequences, and that she's prepared to go out and work if it comes to that."

"A matter of *your* soul?" Philipp said, looking at Nägelsbach as if he had gone mad. "What about *my* soul?"

Nägelsbach looked at him despondently. "I've spent my life making sure that people are called to account for their actions. I can't suddenly—"

"The law doesn't expect you to go to the police or see to it that Welker is charged," I cut in. "You can be on the level with the law if you don't go."

"But you know what I mean," Nägelsbach replied.

Philipp got up, hit his palm against his forehead, and left the room.

Nägelsbach doesn't play chess, so I had brought along my *Othello* board game.

"Shall we play?" I asked him.

We sat down and laid out the double-sided pieces along the grid, flipping them from their white sides to their black sides and back. When that game was over, we played a second game in silence, and then another.

"I do see your point," I told Nägelsbach. "I also see what your wife is saying. There is, by the way, another good reason to go to the police: Do you remember the man who came to your retirement party unannounced and wanted to talk to me? He's been watching us, and there's a good chance he might be out to blackmail us—though probably Welker rather than you, Philipp, or me."

"I don't remember seeing him at my party," Nägelsbach said, smiling with a touch of embarrassment. "I admit I had a glass or two too many."

"Of the three of us, I have the least to lose if you go to the police. Involuntary manslaughter, because we let Welker take Samarin's pistol. We could explain the sequence of events, though I guess it would sound quite contrived. But unlike you or Philipp, I wouldn't be facing disciplinary proceedings. Not to mention that for a private investigator our escapade would not generate negative publicity: quite the opposite. For a retired police officer, though, and for a surgeon at the municipal hospital, it's another matter altogether. So don't worry on my account. But three of us were involved in this—we planned it, set it up, and carried it out. So it's only fair that we three come to a decision as to whether we will inform the police or not. I'd say you either have to convince Philipp that that's the way to go or you'll have to live with the fact that Welker won't be charged."

I waited, but Nägelsbach didn't say anything. He lay there with his eyes shut.

"As for Welker's justification for shooting Samarin," I continued, "I think he's right: Samarin would never have left him alone. In the long run, neither the police nor the law would have managed to protect Welker from Samarin. There's no way they could have. You know that as well as I do."

He slowly opened his eyes. "I'm going to have to give this some thought. I—"

"I want to say one more thing about the soul," I said. "You won't compromise your soul if, for once, you aren't level in a matter concerning you and the law. If you're always on the level, you don't need a soul. We have a soul so we can look at ourselves in the mirror, even when we think we can't. I don't like corrupt policemen. But I know some who at one time or another didn't stick to the book, and who then had a rough time of it but got over it, and precisely because of that became fine policemen. Policemen with a lot of soul."

"I know such policemen, too. But I must admit I always looked down on them a little." He propped himself up in bed and with a sweeping gesture pointed at the room, the empty space for a second bed, the TV, the telephone, and the flowers, and made a stab at a joke. "You see, I, too, am corruptible. I could never pay for all of this. Welker's paying."

10

Like a new case

That evening I sat in my office writing a letter to Vera Soboda, saying that there would be no more money laundering at Weller & Welker; that the bank had been a madhouse in which the patients locked up the doctors and the nurses and were passing themselves off as doctors and nurses; that Samarin, their leader, was dead; and that the institution was once again being run by its doctor, Welker. I liked Nägelsbach's metaphor.

I found a letter from Welker in the mail. He thanked me with a check for twelve thousand marks. He also invited me to a party the Saturday after next to celebrate his move back to the Gustav Kirchhoff Strasse—it would be a pleasant opportunity for us all to meet again.

I wondered whether I should draw up a detailed invoice for him, as I had promised when I took on the case. I usually also submit a written report to my clients once a case is closed. But was the case closed? My client wasn't expecting anything more from me. He had thanked me, paid me, and the convivial get-together to which he was inviting me would also serve as a farewell party. As far as he was concerned, the case was closed. But was it, as far as I was concerned?

Who had frightened Schuler to death? Samarin had neither admitted it nor denied it. I couldn't believe that he got rid of Schuler just because of the money; otherwise, he wouldn't have mentioned that Schuler taught him to read and write. If Samarin had killed him, or had him killed, there was more behind it than the attaché case with the money. But what? And by what means had Schuler been frightened to death?

Or was I on the wrong track? Could it be that *I* didn't want to accept that I was the reason for Schuler's death? Was I looking for a plot when it was nothing more than Schuler's infirmity and disorientation, and my slowness to react? A weak constitution, a bad day, a perplexing amount of money—wasn't that enough to put Schuler into the state he was in when I met him?

I got up and walked over to the window. His Isetta had been parked over there, he had given me the attaché case over there, and then had driven in a long, crooked line across the street and onto the grassy island between the traffic light and the tree. He had died at that tree. The light turned red, yellow, green, and then yellow and red again. I couldn't take my eyes away: the funeral lights of the teacher Adolf Schuler, retired.

Regardless of whether Samarin had frightened him to

death or if his advanced years had gotten him into such a state, I could have saved him but didn't. I owed him. I couldn't do anything about his death now. All I could do was to throw light on it. It was like a new case.

Red, yellow, green, yellow, red. I owed it not only to Schuler to clear up his death but also to myself to solve my last case. Which in fact it was: my last case. I hadn't had one in months when this one came along thanks to a chance encounter on the Hirschhorner Höhe. Perhaps I might be sent out again to investigate people filing false claims for sick leave. But I wouldn't want to do such a job anymore.

It's a shame one can't choose one's last case. A high point, a finale, one that rounds off with a flourish everything one has achieved. Instead, the last case is as accidental as all the others. That's how it goes: you do this, you do that, and before you know it, that was your life.

11

A thousand and one reasons

I ran into Philipp in the corridor. "I'd be happy if I didn't have to go back in there," he said, nodding toward Nägelsbach's room.

"Did you get the forensics report?"

"The forensics report?" Then he remembered what I wanted and that the report was lying on his desk. "Come with me."

Both chairs in front of his desk were heaped high with files and mail, so I sat down on his examination table, as if he were going to come over and tap my knee with a little hammer to check my reflexes. He leafed through the report. "Schuler:

chest and stomach crushed, vital organs damaged, neck broken. It was a bad accident."

"I was with him just minutes before it happened. Something was wrong with him. It was as if someone had frightened the living daylights out of him."

"Perhaps he was sick. Perhaps he'd taken too many sleeping pills. Perhaps his medications interacted. Perhaps he had an adverse reaction to a new sedative or blood-pressure medication. By God, Gerhard, there are a thousand and one reasons why someone might be in a bad state and have an accident."

But I just couldn't believe that Schuler could have taken the wrong blood-pressure medication or too many sleeping pills. He was no fool. The piles of books and folders seemed chaotic but were in meticulous order, and surely his medications would have been, too.

"There's also the matter of—" Philipp began insistently.

"What if I track down the medications he was taking?" I cut in. "If I locate his doctor, could you give him a call?"

"What could his doctor tell us?"

"I have no idea. Maybe he did prescribe a new medication that backfired. Or maybe Schuler got some pills on his own, and the doctor could confirm that whatever he'd taken interfered with the medication he'd been prescribed. His doctor could even tell us whether he had a strawberry allergy and that someone might have made him eat a strawberry, or that he had asthma and might have had a fatal shock during an attack when he realized that someone had taken away his inhaler. If I know what might have frightened him, I'd have a better chance of finding out who it was."

"If you come up with something, I'll see to the rest," Philipp said, trying his best to appear interested. But something else was preoccupying him. "You've got to stop Nägelsbach! You've got to stop him before it's too late. I haven't told you this, because I don't believe in counting my chickens before they're hatched, but I've been put forward for the directorship of the surgical department of an absolutely first-rate private clinic. Right now I need disciplinary proceedings like I need a bullet in the head."

"I thought your retirement was in the works."

"I'll be retiring soon enough. But private clinics are more flexible when it comes to retirement age. Tending flowers on my balcony from morning to night and moving my boat around isn't my cup of tea. And the nurses at the new clinic . . . Imagine, a chance to start all over again from scratch! And then the thought of working somewhere where Füruzan can't keep an eye on me and frighten off all the other nurses! I wouldn't be surprised if the only reason I feel like an old circus horse is because Füruzan's never more than half a step away."

"I've already had a word with Nägelsbach," I said.

"His soul, his soul . . . My soul will go to the dogs if I no longer have my hospital!"

He looked at me in utter desperation. What did women find so attractive in Philipp? Was it that when he was in a certain mood, he was in every way totally in it?

"Even if you don't like the idea of facing Nägelsbach," I said, "if you want something from him, you've got to talk to him yourself."

"I'm no good at that sort of thing."

"Give it a try. He's not stiff-necked—he's just extremely conscientious. But he'll take whatever you say very seriously."

"I'll make a scene, even if I'd rather not," Philipp said sadly. "The nurses like it when I start bellowing at them, but Nägelsbach won't." He glanced at the clock and got up. "I've got to move on. What do you think—will Nägelsbach play along?"

"He'll either go straight to the police when he's discharged or he won't go at all. But before he goes he'll tell us. You'll have to wait till he's discharged."

Philipp laughed and shook his head as if I ought to know better. "Do you expect me to wait that long?"

12

Traveling

I went to Schwetzingen and knocked on the doors of Schuler's neighbors, asking them for his niece's address, until one of them sent me to the Werkstrasse, beyond the railroad tracks.

There the garden gate stood open, and a note on the door said Frau Schubert would be right back. I waited. In the yard across the street some garden gnomes were being given a bath in a zinc tub, plunged into the water dirty sad, emerging happy and clean.

Frau Schubert came riding up on her bicycle.

"Oh, hello! I'll make us some coffee," she called out.

I helped her carry her groceries inside. The deliveryman for whom she had left the note on the door appeared, and I carried in the cases of beer, lemonade, and soft drinks that he unloaded at the gate. By the time I finished, the coffee was ready.

Frau Schubert struck me as being a little embarrassed.

"I didn't remember your name," she said, "so I couldn't send you a death notice. Is that why you dropped by? The burial will be next week, on Tuesday."

I promised her that I would attend, and she invited me to the reception after the service. I told her that I had lent her uncle some books that I needed, and she offered to drive me to his house so I could look for them. As we drove there, she told me about the offer she had gotten for her uncle's library.

"Imagine. Fifteen thousand marks!"

"Are you his sole heir?" I asked.

"He didn't have any children, and my cousin died a few years ago in a hang-gliding accident. I'm inheriting his house, though it will need so much work that I'd be very happy to get fifteen thousand for the books."

I can't tell what old books are worth, but as I looked around Schuler's house I saw that he had amassed a rather unusual library. On the one hand, he had collected books about the area between Edingen and Waghäusel, and on the other, books about railways and banks in Baden. I couldn't imagine that there would be anything published on these topics that wouldn't be here. Most of the publications were small pamphlets, but there were also thick linen- and leather-bound volumes among them, at times whole series of works from the nineteenth century. About the channeling of the Rhine and the stabilization of its meadows by Major Tulla, the viaducts and tunnels of the railroad of the Odenwald Range, or the river police on the Rhine and the Neckar, from their founding until today. I resisted the temptation to claim as one of the books I'd lent Schuler a volume concerning the details of the construction of the Bismarck Tower on the Heiligenberg.

The cabinet above the sink in the bathroom was packed with medicines: pills for heart and blood pressure, insomnia, headaches, constipation, and diarrhea; pills for strengthening the prostate and calming the vegetative nervous system; ointments for varicose veins and rheumatism; corn plasters and corn scrapers. Many medicines were duplicated, and many had expired. Some of the tubes had dried out, and some of the pills that had once been white were now yellow. I ignored the scrapers, plasters, and ointments, the constipation and diarrhea pills, and the strengthening and invigorating medicines. But I took with me the tranquilizers, the sleeping pills, and the heart and blood-pressure pills—seven in all. The cabinet was still full enough for their absence not to be noticed.

Frau Schubert had opened all the windows and the spring air battled with Schuler's smell. The kitchen no longer stank of rotting food but of lemony detergent. A sparkling cleanliness had settled in.

"You didn't find your books?" Frau Schubert said, seeing me come out of the study empty-handed.

"I gave up. Your uncle had too many books."

She nodded sympathetically, but also with some pride.

"Just like with his medicines," I added. "He simply had too many. I had to use the bathroom, and noticed it was filled with them."

"He couldn't bring himself to throw anything away. And also, he liked those old medicines, the ones that came in little bottles. With his gouty fingers he couldn't open the new plastic or aluminum packets. I always had to take out the pills and put them in little bottles for him." She wiped a tear from her eye.

"Who was his doctor?"

"Dr. Armbrust in Luisenstrasse."

As we walked to the front door we passed the wall where Schuler had hung his photographs. One was of him as a young man with a broad grin standing next to his Isetta, his hand resting on the car like a general's resting on his map table. We looked at the photographs until Frau Schubert began crying again.

I called Philipp from the phone booth in the Hebelstrasse, the one Welker had not wanted to use. "It's Dr. Armbrust in the Luisenstrasse in Schwetzingen."

"Oh, come on, Gerhard." It was clear I was getting on his nerves. But he gave in. "Okay, I'll call him right away."

When I called Philipp back a little while later, he told me that Dr. Armbrust was on vacation for three weeks. "Will you get off my back now?"

"Can't you call him at home?" I asked. "Who knows whether he's gone anywhere."

"You mean—"

"Right away. Yes, call him now."

Philipp sighed, but he found the number. "Stay on the line; I'll call him on my cell phone."

Dr. Armbrust wasn't at home, either. His housekeeper explained that he'd be traveling till the last day of his vacation.

13

Apple pie and cappuccino

Ulbrich came by on Sunday afternoon. He no longer held my refusal to be his father against me. I once read somewhere that East Germans have a taste for the finer things in life, so on Saturday I had baked an apple pie. He ate a piece with pleasure and asked for some chocolate sprinkles for the whipped cream I had made so he could turn his cup of coffee into a cappuccino. Turbo let Ulbrich cuddle him, and I can't imagine things having been any cozier back in the old Socialist days.

I had selected some photographs of Klara for him to look at. There are five albums on my shelf: one with pictures of Klara as a baby and little girl with her brother and parents;

one with Klara as a beautiful tennis and ski debutante, one devoted to our engagement, marriage, and honeymoon; and one to our last months in Berlin and our first years in Heidelberg. All these albums make me sad. The one that makes me saddest is the last album, of the postwar period and the fifties and sixties. Klara, who had dreamed of a sparkling life at the side of a public prosecutor with a glittering career, and in these dreams had herself glittered and sparkled, had had to readjust her sights to a scrimping reality and had become increasingly bitter. Back then I had held her bitterness and reproaches against her. I simply could no longer be a public prosecutor, first because I was no longer wanted on account of my past in the Third Reich, but also because I resisted, body and soul, acting with my colleagues as if we had no past, even if we were expected to. So I had become a private investigator. Couldn't she accept that? Couldn't she love me as I was? I have come to realize that love can be as much a matter of the expression, the laughter, the wit, the intelligence, or the other one's caring as it can be a matter of his standing in the world and his circumstances. Would she have been a happy mother? After giving birth to Karl-Heinz Ulbrich, she could no longer have children; during his birth something must have gone wrong.

But you couldn't tell just by looking at her. She was laughing in the photograph of April 1942, which I'd taken outside our house in the Bahnhofstrasse after her so-called Italian trip with Gigi. And again in a picture from June 1941, where she is walking along Unter den Linden and comes across as cheerful. Had the other man taken this picture? I had also brought out a picture from her school days, one from the 1950s where she was finally playing tennis again, since I was once more earning enough, and a picture taken shortly before she died.

Ulbrich looked at the photos slowly, without saying a word. "What did she die of?"

"Cancer."

He assumed a troubled look and shook his head. "It's still not fair though. I mean, once a child is born it also has to . . ." He didn't continue.

What would I have done if Klara had wanted to keep the child? Had she ever asked herself this and concluded that I couldn't have handled something like that?

He shook his head again. "It's all very unfair. What a beautiful woman she was. The man . . . the man must have also been quite handsome. And take a look at me." He held his face toward me as if I'd never seen it before. "If you'd been my father, I could understand. But with two such good-looking people . . ."

I burst out laughing, and he was taken aback. He made himself another cappuccino and had another slice of apple pie.

"I read that article in the *Mannheimer Morgen*. I must say, your police force goes about things quite casually. Back in the East things would have been done very differently. But perhaps things will be done differently here, too, if someone points the police in the right direction." His look was no longer sad but defiant, the way he had looked at me when we first met. Could it be that today he wasn't so disappointed in me because he felt he had the upper hand?

I didn't say anything.

"You haven't really done anything. But the other guy, the one from the bank . . ." He waited, and when I was still silent, he continued feeling his way forward. "I mean, he clearly preferred not to tell the police that he . . . And I imagine that he'd also prefer that nobody else would tell them that—"

"You would tell them?"

"You needn't say that so sharply, as if I were some . . . All I'm saying is, he'd do better not to leave anything to chance. Are you still working for him?"

Did he intend to blackmail Welker?

"Are you in such bad financial shape?" I asked him.

"I—"

"You'd do better to go back where you came from. I'm sure the security network will soon be flourishing there the way it is everywhere else. Firms will be looking for representatives, and insurance companies will be looking for agents who know their way around. There's nothing for you to gain here. It'll be your word against ours—how far will you get?"

"My word? What do you think I'm going to say? I was only asking. I mean . . . ," After a while he said quietly: "I tried to get a job as a security guard, and also as an insurance agent, even as a zookeeper. It's not that easy."

"That's a pity."

He nodded. "There are no free rides anymore."

After he left I called Welker. I wanted to warn him. Should Ulbrich seek him out, I didn't want him to find Welker unprepared. "Thank you for informing me," he said. He took down Ulbrich's name and address and seemed quite unruffled. "See you next Saturday."

14

One and one that makes two

The children enjoyed Welker's party most. They were the right age—Manu and Welker's son, Max, were a little older than Isabel, Welker's daughter, and Anne, the daughter of Füruzan's colleague who had taken part in the operation at the water tower. At first the boys sat at the computer, ignoring the girls, who went to another room and dolled themselves up. Brigitte crinkled her nose—she'd rather have seen them at the computer than falling into the beauty trap. But once the girls were all prettied up the boys forgot about the computer and began to flirt. Manu with Isabel, who had inherited the dark hair and fiery eyes of her mother, and Max with Anne, both blond. The garden was large, and when Brigitte and I took a walk over to the pear tree by the fence, we saw that one of the teen couples was making out on the bench beneath the blackthorn, and the other couple was sitting on the wall by the roses. It was a sweet and innocent sight. Still, Brigitte was worried when it got dark and the children didn't come to the table that had been set up in the garden, so she went looking for them. They were sitting on the balcony drinking Coca-Cola and eating potato chips and talking about love and death.

The Nägelsbachs were there, along with Philipp and Füruzan, Füruzan's colleague and her boyfriend, and Brigitte and me. I could see how relieved Philipp was that Nägelsbach had decided not to go to the police. There was also a young woman there whom Welker introduced as Max's teacher at the Kurfürst-Friedrich Gymnasium and on whom he lavished as much attention as a young widower with two children could afford to. I've forgotten who the other guests were. They were Welker's neighbors and friends, or acquaintances from his tennis club.

At first the conversation was a little stiff, but the awkwardness quickly evaporated. The wine, a chardonnay from the Palatine, went down so easily, the food was so simple and convincing—from thick green spelt soup and Victoria perch to blackberry trifle—and the glow of candles was so cozy. Welker gave a little speech; he was happy to be reunited with his children. He thanked the water tower commandos—though he preferred not to touch on why he had been away or what he was thanking us for. But everyone was pleased.

It grew cooler, and a fireplace was glowing inside the house.

"Shall we go for a stroll in the garden before we go inside?" Welker said, taking me aside.

We crossed the lawn and sat down on a bench beneath the blackthorn.

"I've thought a lot about Gregor Samarin—and us Welkers, too. We took him in, but everything we gave him was like a handout. Because we gave, we also expected his services. When I was a boy I had the room in the attic, while his room was in the cellar so he could take care of the central heating, which back then still ran on coal, not oil." He slowly shook his head. "I've been trying to remember when I first realized that he hated me. I can't recall. Back then it simply didn't interest me, which is why I can't remember." He looked at me. "Isn't that terrible?"

I nodded.

"I know that shooting him was even worse," Welker continued. "But somehow it's terrible in the same way. Do you know what I mean? What happened in our childhood bore fruit, as the Bible says. In his case, it was murdering my wife and everything else he did, and in my case, that I could only save myself from him the way I did."

"He told me he liked your wife."

"He liked Stephanie the way a servant might like the daughter of a master he hates. At the end of the day her place is on the other side, and when the chips are down, that's all that matters. When Stephanie confronted him, the chips were down."

The lights went on in the house and their glow fell on the lawn. It remained dark beneath the blackthorn. Someone put on a Hildegard Knef record: "One and One That Makes Two." I wanted to take Brigitte in my arms and dance a waltz.

"As for Stephanie," he continued, "I don't know where it

was that they . . . Were they waiting for her up at the hut? I have no idea how they could have followed us without our noticing. We thought we were alone." He pressed his hands against his eyes and sighed. "I still can't rid myself of this nightmare. And yet all I want is to wake up and put it all behind me."

I felt sorry for him. At the same time, I didn't really want to hear what he was telling me. I wasn't his friend. I had completed the case he had hired me for. I now had another case.

"What did you talk about with Schuler the evening you went to see him?" I asked.

"Schuler . . ." If I had hurt him by the abrupt change of topic, he showed no sign. "Gregor and I went to see him together. He told us about his work with the files and about the Strasbourg lead concerning the silent partner, which you later followed. Otherwise . . ."

"Did you ask him for the money? The money in the attaché case?"

"He talked about it, but back then I wasn't quite sure what it was all about. Schuler said that a person becomes suspicious when he finds money in a cellar and starts wondering whom it might belong to, knowing that no good comes of evil, and had we forgotten that? He was looking at Gregor when he said it."

"What did you—"

"I wasn't there the whole time. I had . . . I had diarrhea and kept having to go to the toilet. Schuler must have found the money Gregor had stashed away in a part of the old cellar, where he had no business being. He put two and two together and suspected Gregor, because I am a Welker and Gregor doesn't belong to the family. He wanted to get his former pupil back on the straight and narrow." Welker laughed with a touch of mockery and sadness. "I suppose you'll also want to know what state Schuler was in. He smelled bad, but he was fine. Furthermore, he didn't make any threats. He didn't even say that he had the money. Gregor found that out the next day."

Hildegard Knef's song had ended. I heard applause, laughter, voices, and then the song was played again, louder this time. If I couldn't take part in the dancing, I'd at least have liked to sing along: "God in Heaven is all-seeing, he's seen right through you, there's no point in fleeing."

Welker laid his hand on my knee. "I won't ever forget what you did for me. One day, thank God, the memories of the last few months will pale. Until now the good things that have happened to me have remained clearer in my mind than the bad, and what you did for me as my private investigator was a good thing." He got up. "Shall we go inside?"

When Hildegard Knef sang the song for a third time, I danced with Brigitte.

PART THREE

I

Too *late*

Why couldn't things stay as they were? Light, cheerful, and breezy, with a little sadness and a little mourning—mourning for Stephanie Welker, Adolf Schuler, and Gregor Samarin. Yes, for Gregor Samarin, too, destructive as his life had been. And sadness, because Brigitte and I only now discovered the lightness with which our feet found the right steps as we moved in harmony and enjoyed each other. Why couldn't we dance like this through the whole year, this year, next year, the one after, and as many years as we would have?

I saw the same happiness I felt on the faces of the others. The Nägelsbachs smiled as if they were sharing a precious secret; Philipp's face no longer showed his peevishness at growing old; and Füruzan's face no longer showed the weariness of her long path from Anatolia to Germany and all the many nights during which she earned the money that she sent back home. Brigitte was beaming, as if finally everything were fine. Welker wasn't dancing. He was leaning with folded arms against the door frame watching us with a friendly smile, as if waiting for us to leave. We left when it started getting late for the children.

A few days after the party Brigitte and I went to Sardinia. Manu's school was on vacation, and to everyone's surprise Manu's father announced that he was taking Manu skiing. Brigitte, who hadn't anticipated her ex-husband's plan, hadn't scheduled any appointments at her massage practice so she wouldn't be working during Manu's break. She said to me: "It's now or never." That's how far things had come—*her* calendar would dictate what we would or wouldn't do; mine didn't count.

Ten days in Sardinia. We'd never spent so much time together. Our hotel was past its heyday; in the lobby the dark red leather of the armchairs and sofas was frayed, the candelabras in the dining room were no longer lit, and the brass fittings in the bathroom spewed out rusty water when we first turned on the faucets. But we were attentively served and looked after. The hotel stood among the trees of an overgrown garden on a small pebble-beach bay, and whether we decided to linger in the garden or by the water, the staff was quick to bring us two loungers, a table, and a beach umbrella if needed, and they were eager to serve us espresso, water, Campari, or Sardinian white wine.

The first days we did nothing but lounge about, blinking through the leaves at the sun and gazing dreamily over the sea to the horizon. Then we rented a car and drove along the coast and up into the mountains over narrow, winding roads to small villages with churches and market squares and vistas of valleys that at times stretched all the way to the sea. Old men sat in the squares, and I would have liked to sit with them and hear their tales of what dangerous brigands they used to be, tell them what a capable detective I had once been, and parade Brigitte before them. In Cagliari we climbed interminable steps up to the terrace of the Bastione and looked down at the harbor and the motley rooftops. In a small harbor town there was a feast with a procession and a chorus and orchestra that played and sang so heartrendingly that Brigitte's eyes welled with tears. The last days we again spent lying on the beach under the trees.

It was in Sardinia that I fell in love with Brigitte. I know it sounds foolish; we'd been together for years, and what tied me to her if not love? But it was in Sardinia that my eyes were opened. How beautiful Brigitte was when she wasn't stressed out and didn't have to worry. How gracefully she walked— light of foot but also with a certain determined step. What a wonderful mother she was to Manu, and what trust she had in him in spite of her many worries. How witty she could be. How charmingly she linked her arm in mine. How lovingly she handled my ways and peculiarities. How she massaged my back when it hurt. How she brought brightness and cheer into my life.

I tried to recall the longings she had sometimes talked of and strove to fulfill them. To say something nice from time to time for no particular reason, to give her flowers, to read something to her, to come up with something fun that we hadn't done yet, to surprise her with a bottle of wine she had enjoyed in a restaurant, or to buy her a handbag that had caught her eye in the window of a boutique. They were all minor things, and I was ashamed that like an old cheapskate I had withheld them from her for so long.

The days flew by. I had taken some books with me, but didn't finish any of them. As I lay on the lounger I preferred to watch Brigitte reading instead of reading myself. Or I watched her sleep and wake up. Sometimes she didn't know right away where she was. She saw the blue sky and the blue sea and was a little confused until she remembered, and then she smiled at me sleepily and happily.

I happily smiled back. But I was also sad. Again I had been too slow—something that shouldn't have taken more than a few weeks or months had taken years. And because I have always realized that I've been too slow at a point when I've irrevocably missed a chance or lost something through my slowness, now, too, I had the feeling that it was too late for our happiness.

2

Matthew 25: 14–30

Manu returned from his ski trip with a deep tan and delighted Brigitte by saying, "But it's great to be back again." He surprised me by announcing that he wanted to go to church the following morning. During the ski trip his father had taken him to mass, as he also used to do in Brazil. His mother had never taken him to church here.

So on Sunday I went with him to the Christuskirche. The sun was shining, and around the water tower narcissus and tulips "bloomed in greater splendor than all the silks of Solomon can render." The golden angel with the golden trumpet greeted us from the top of the church cupola. I was struck by what the priest had said about the parable in which the servant buries the money that has been entrusted to him instead of putting it to work, thus dodging his responsibility. What was I intending to do with the money I had buried under the potted palm? Drop it in the collection box? It had slipped my mind.

Manu, too, had been listening attentively to the sermon. Over lunch he told Brigitte and me that his friend had a brother who was a few years older and who was increasing his money by buying and selling stocks on the Internet. Manu gleaned from that and from Matthew 25: 14–30, that either his mother or his father ought to get him a computer. Then he looked at me. "Or will you?"

That afternoon we went to Schwetzingen and visited the palace gardens, which I had so often seen from a distance while I was working on my case. We walked down the avenue that looked so new with its young chestnut trees, past the orangerie and to the Roman aqueduct, over the Chinese bridge, and along the lake to the Temple of Mercury. Brigitte showed us where her parents had hidden Easter eggs for her and her brothers and sisters. At the mosque Manu declared, "Allah leads to the light whom He wills!"—which he'd learned at school when the class had an assignment on Islam. Then we sat down in the sun on the Schlossplatz and had some coffee and cake. I recognized the waitress, but she didn't recognize me. I looked across the way to Weller & Welker.

Locals and tourists were strolling over the Schlossplatz, which was bustling with life. A dark Saab slowly and patiently made its way through the throng. It stopped in front of the bank. The gate swung open and the car drove in.

That was all. A car stops in front of the gate, the gate swings open and stays open for a moment, the car enters, and the gate closes again. This was not the image that had stayed in my mind from the afternoon when I had watched the bank for the first time. Back then the square had been empty, while today it was full. Back then the cars that entered and exited the bank gate were not to be overlooked, while today the dark Saab was almost swallowed up in the hustle and bustle of the square.

But it struck me like an electric shock. You insert the key into the lock of your car or turn on the radio, or you step out onto the balcony, perhaps in your pajamas and dressing gown, to check the temperature and take a look at the sky, and you lean on the metal railing. The static shock barely hurts. What strikes you is not the pain, but the sudden realization that the car, the radio, the railing—everything we are so familiar with and rely on—also has an unreliable, malignant side to it. That things are not as reliable as we suppose them to be. The car entering and the opening and closing of the gate! Just like back then, I had the feeling that something was not quite right in what was happening before my eyes.

A client on a Sunday? I couldn't rule that out for a small bank and an important client. But the one business that would not rest on a weekend or holiday was money laundering.

When the gate opened again half an hour later, letting the dark Saab out and then closed, I was standing nearby. The car had a Frankfurt license plate. The windows were tinted. A fifty-mark bill that had fallen out during the delivery was peeking out from the edge of the trunk.

When I told Brigitte that evening in bed that I would be out of town for a few days, she asked wryly: "So, the lone cowboy is riding silently into the setting sun?"

"The cowboy is riding to Cottbus, and into the rising sun,

not the setting sun. And he isn't riding silently, either." I told her about the money laundering at the Sorbian Cooperative Bank and that I wanted to find out if it was still going on. I told her about Vera Soboda. I told her about Schuler and his money. "The money came from the East and has to go back to the East. Perhaps I can find a priest or some institution that can put it to good use. And perhaps I will find something that will help throw some light on Schuler's death."

Brigitte rested her head on her hands and looked up at the ceiling. "*I* could put the money to good use. What I'd like to do instead of my massage practice, what I would need to expand my practice, things Manu would like—I could definitely put it to good use."

"It's drug money, and money from prostitution and blackmail. It's dirty money. I'll be happy when it's gone."

"Money doesn't stink—weren't you taught that?"

I propped myself on my elbow and looked at Brigitte. After a while she turned her eyes from the ceiling and looked at me.

I didn't like her expression. "Come on, Brigitte . . ." I didn't know what to say.

"Maybe that's why you are what you are. A lonely, difficult old man. You don't see happiness when it comes your way, so how are you supposed to grab it if you can't even see it? Here it's served to you on a silver platter, but you let it slip away. Just like you've let our happiness slip away." She looked back up at the ceiling.

"I don't want our happiness to—"

"I know you don't want to, Gerhard, but you do it anyway."

I couldn't let that go. I wasn't ready to roll over and turn my back to her, lonely, difficult, and old. Not after our days in Sardinia.

"Brigitte?"

"Yes?"

"What would you rather do instead of your massage practice?"

She was silent for so long that I thought she wasn't going to say anything more. Then she wept a few tears. "I would have liked to have had children with you. I had Manu despite my sterilization. I didn't have any with you, though I didn't take any precautions. We would have had to try it in vitro."

"You and me in a test tube?"

"You think the doctor will shake us up in a test tube like a barman with a cocktail shaker? He would lay your sperm and my egg on a glass slide and then let them do what people in love do in bed."

I liked the idea of the two cells on a glass. It was a pleasant image.

"Now it's too late," Brigitte said.

"I'm sorry. I just told you about Schuler. He would still be alive if I hadn't been too slow. I've always been too slow, and not just since I've grown older. I should have asked you after our first night together whether you wanted to marry me."

I reached out my hand, and after a slight hesitation Brigitte raised her head and I slid my arm under it.

"It's not too late for that."

"Do you want to?"

"Yes." She nestled up to me and nodded.

"First I have to finish this case. It'll be my last case."

3

Stealing tractors

This time I avoided Berlin. I went by car, got off the autobahn at Weimar and meandered over back roads. There was a park before Cottbus that had been created by Count Pückler, with a pyramid for himself and his wife, one for his favorite horse, and one for his favorite dog. The count's Egyptian girlfriend had to make do with a grave in the cemetery. She had been young, beautiful, and dark, but her delicate Middle Eastern lungs couldn't bear the Sorbian climate. I understood her. I hadn't been able to stand up to the Sorbian climate on my last visit, either.

I had called Vera Soboda at her home in the morning and she'd invited me to dinner. She made a local potato dish with curd and offered me some Lausitzer Urquell, a beer from the region that has a sharp tang of hops but is easy on the palate.

"What brings you to Cottbus?" she asked.

"The Sorbian bank. Do you know how I can get at the data you told me about last time?"

"I don't work there anymore. I was fired." She laughed. "Don't look so surprised. I wasn't actually the bank manager. I just ran everything because someone had to do it, and the position had never been filled. Two weeks ago some idiot who knows nothing about banking was made manager. On his third day he fired me. It was all over in a flash. He came up to my desk and said: 'Frau Soboda, you are fired. You have half an hour to remove any personal items from your desk and to leave the premises.' He stood beside me and watched me, as if I might take the hole-puncher, the paper clips, or a pen. Then he walked me to the door and said: 'You will receive seven months' pay. Fair is fair.'"

"Did you see a lawyer?"

"The lawyer only shook his head and said my chances were up in the air. It seems I might have spoken my mind a little too clearly to the new manager. So I let it be. We have no experience here in taking employers to court. Were I to lose, who'd pay for it all?"

"What are you going to do now?"

"There's enough to do around here. The problem is that what we need in these parts doesn't generate money, and what generates money, we more often than not don't need. But everything will fall into place. Our Lord in Heaven will not abandon a good Communist, as my former boss who took me under her wing always used to say."

I was certain she would make it. She again looked like a

tractor driver with whom one would gladly set out to steal tractors. She furrowed her brow. "What kind of data are you looking for?"

"I'd like to know if money's still being laundered."

"But you wrote me that—"

"I know. It's just that I'm not sure if what I wrote you was right. I have a feeling that—"

"Do you know your way around computers?"

"No."

She got up, placed her hands on her hips, and looked me up and down. "Do you expect me to go prowling with you through the night, break into the Sorbian bank, turn on the computer, and sift through it for data, just because you have 'a feeling'? You expect me to risk my neck for this feeling of yours? Do you think I'll get so much as a cleaning job in a bank if I'm caught at the Sorbian? Are you out of your mind?" She stood there scolding me in a way that I hadn't been scolded since the days my mother used to tell me off. If I'd stood up I'd have towered over her by a head, ruining the magic. So I remained seated and stared at her enthusiastically until she stopped, sat down, and burst out laughing.

"Did I say anything about breaking in?"

"No," she replied, still laughing. "I said it. And I'd like nothing more than to do it and give those programs and databases a good whirl. But I can't. Not even with you, who didn't say anything about breaking in, but thought about it."

"How about without you? Could I get inside without you and turn the computer on and look for the data?"

"Didn't you just say you don't know anything about computers?"

"Can't you lay out for me what you did back then? Step by step? I—"

"You want to become a hacker in a single day? Forget it."

"I—"

"It's almost eleven, and we Sorbians go to bed early. Let's have another beer, and then I'll fix you up on the sofa."

4

In the broom closet

"Theoretically speaking," I said to Vera Soboda over breakfast, "is there a way of getting into the Sorbian bank under
cover of darkness?"

She answered so quickly that she, too, must have given this
some thought overnight.

"Under cover of darkness is not the time to break in. What
you would have to do is unlock the door to the kitchen area
with a skeleton key in the afternoon and hide in the broom
closet until everyone's gone. Then you would have the bank
to yourself. Getting in isn't hard—it's getting out. At seven in
the morning, when the cleaning ladies show up, you would

have to hide again until the bank opened, when you could mingle with the customers. But you couldn't hide in the closet, because that's where the detergents and mops are kept, and the ladies will be cleaning the toilets, the room with the copiers, behind the tellers' counters, and under the desks. And you can't get into the room that has the deposit boxes and the safe."

"How do the cleaning ladies get into the bank?"

"They have a key for the side entrance."

"Could I tear past them when they unlock the door?"

She gave the idea some thought. We were having eggs and bacon with potatoes, along with bread and jam and coffee. She ate as if she hadn't eaten in ages and wouldn't eat again in ages. When I gave up at my second egg, she ate what was left on my plate, too.

"Eat breakfast like a bishop, lunch like a priest, dinner like a mendicant," she said. "The cleaning ladies would get the fright of their lives and call the police. But why not?"

She wiped both plates clean with a piece of bread.

"Shall we continue theorizing a little?" I asked.

She laughed. "No harm in that, I suppose."

"If you were in the bank, sitting at the computer, and couldn't figure out the programs and the data but happened to have a cell phone handy with which you could call someone who knew what was what, wouldn't you then—"

She laughed again, her belly shaking as she steadied herself on the table as if she would fall off her chair if she didn't. I waited for her to calm down.

"Frau Soboda, can you show me on your computer what I would have to do tonight? And would you help me if I got stuck and called you on a cell phone? I know there isn't much chance I'll find anything, but I won't rest if I don't at least give it a try."

She looked at the clock. "In six hours," she said. "Do you have a cell phone?"

She directed me to a store where I could get one. When I returned, she sat down with me at her computer. She showed and explained; I asked and practiced. Turning the computer on. Entering the password. What could the right password be? How did one switch from the system to the tracking program? How would I locate the accounts in the system and the tracking program? What routes might lead to the money laundering? How would I describe on the cell phone what was happening on the screen? By three o'clock I no longer knew up from down.

"You still have a few hours to think the whole procedure through again. The new manager tends to stay late, and I wouldn't recommend your coming out of the broom closet before eight." She explained how I should smuggle myself into the bank's kitchen area and said, "Good luck!"

I parked my car on a side street and went into the Sorbian bank. I was to walk past the tellers and the cashier and enter a short hallway at the beginning of which were the restrooms and the kitchen area. It was quite straightforward. Nobody noticed me as I slowly made my way past the busy tellers and, in the hallway, quickly unlocked the door to the kitchen area with my skeleton key and pulled it shut behind me.

The closet was full. I had to rearrange the brooms, mops, buckets, and detergents so that I'd have enough space. It was uncomfortable; I had to stand at attention with the fuse box pressing into my back, my feet locked together, and my hands at my sides. There was a powerful smell of detergent—not the aroma of fresh lemons but a mixture of soap, ammonia, and rotting fruit. At first I left the closet door ajar, certain I would hear anyone approaching the kitchen. But when someone did come in, I noticed him only once he was already in the room, and if he had looked in my direction that would have been the end of me. So I shut the door. When the bank closed at four, the kitchen area livened up. The employees who had worked at the tellers' counters and now had to tally their accounts all took a coffee break. I heard the coffeemaker hissing and gurgling, cups and spoons clattering, comments about customers, and gossip about colleagues. I felt quite uneasy in the closet. But time flew.

Otherwise it dragged on slowly. At first I went through what I had learned about the computer. But soon I could think of nothing but how to inch my legs into a different position and move my arms so they'd hurt less. I admired the soldiers who stood guard at Buckingham Palace or the Élysée. I also envied them for their spacious sentry boxes. From time to time I heard a sound, but I couldn't tell if it was coming from the banking hall or the street, if a chair had banged against a desk or a car had rear-ended another or a plank had fallen off some scaffolding. Most of the time I heard only the rustling of my blood in my ears and a low, delicate piping noise that didn't come from outside but was also in my ears. I decided that at eight I would climb out of the closet, open the kitchen door, and see if I could hear anything in the banking hall.

But at quarter to eight it was all over. I again heard a sound. While I was still trying to figure out where it was coming from and what it might mean, the kitchen door was abruptly opened. For a moment there was silence. The man who had entered stood still, as if he were running his eyes over the sink, the stove, the refrigerator, the table and chairs, the cabinets above the sink, and the broom closet next to the stove. Then he quickly strode toward the closet and tore open the door.

5

In a dark suit and vest

I was blinded by the light and could see only that someone was standing in front of me. I shut my eyes tightly, opened them wide, and blinked. Then I recognized him. Ulbrich was standing in front of me.

Karl-Heinz Ulbrich, in a dark suit and vest, a pink shirt and red tie, and silver-rimmed spectacles, over which he looked at me with eyes that were doing their best to seem resolute and menacing. "Herr Self."

I laughed. I laughed, because the tension of the last minute and from having stood for so long was dissolving. I laughed at Ulbrich's getup, and at the glare. I laughed at being caught in the broom closet as if I were the lover of the Sorbian bank and Ulbrich her jealous husband.

"Herr Self." He didn't sound resolute and menacing. How could I have forgotten what a sensitive little fellow Ulbrich was? I tried to cap off my laughing in such a way that he might interpret it as me laughing with him, not at him. But it was too late, and he looked at me as if I had hurt his feelings again.

"Herr Self, I wouldn't be laughing if I were you. You have entered these premises illegally."

I nodded. "Yes, Herr Ulbrich. It's me. How did you find me?"

"I saw your car parked on a side street. Where else would you be, if not here?"

"Who'd have thought that someone in Cottbus would recognize my car! But perhaps I ought to have figured out that Welker would send you here as his new bank manager."

"Are you hinting that . . . are you hinting that I . . . Herr Self, your insinuation that I might have blackmailed Herr Welker is an outrage! I protest most vigorously! Director Welker saw my merits, something you cannot claim to have done, and was delighted to put them to good use! Mark my words, he was delighted!"

I got out of the closet, my numb legs knocking over detergent bottles, buckets, and mops. Ulbrich looked at me reproachfully. Why was it that with him I always ended up sooner or later having a bad conscience? I wasn't his father; I could not have let him down as his father. I wasn't his uncle, cousin, or brother, either.

"I understand," I said to him. "You are not blackmailing him. He is delighted that you are working for him. I want to go now."

"You have illegally—"

"You've said that already. Welker doesn't want any fuss in his bank. The police and I would amount to a considerable fuss. I imagine he doesn't even want to know that I spent a few hours in his bank in the company of brooms and buckets. Forget my illegal entry. Forget it and let me go."

He shook his head but then turned around and left the kitchen area. I followed him to the side entrance. He unlocked the door and let me out. I looked up and down the street and heard the door shut behind me and the key turn twice.

The side street was empty. I intended to head over to the old market square, but I went the wrong way and came to a wide street I didn't know. Here, too, there was nobody about. It was a mild evening, perfect for a stroll, for sitting outside, for a chat over wine or beer, for flirting, but the people of Cottbus didn't seem to be in the mood for any of this. I found a little Turkish restaurant with a table and two chairs out on the sidewalk. I ordered a beer and stuffed vine leaves and sat down.

Across the street two boys were messing around with their motorbikes, making the engines roar from time to time. After a while they sped off, riding around the block once, and then again and again. They finally pulled up across the street, their engines running, again making them roar from time to time, and after a while set off around the block once again. This went on and on. They looked like good kids, and what they were yelling to each other was harmless enough. Still, the roar of their bikes ripped violently through the air, like the sound of a dentist's drill. Before you feel it in the tooth, you feel it in the brain.

"You're not from these parts," the owner of the restaurant said, putting the plate, glass, and bottle down in front of me.

I nodded. "How's life here?"

"You can hear for yourself. Never a dull moment."

Before I could ask him any further questions he went inside. There was no knife or fork, so I ate the stuffed vine leaves with my fingers. Then I poured myself a glass.

I didn't think Ulbrich was blackmailing Welker. It was more likely that after I'd warned Welker he had given Ulbrich a call, invited him over, and then hired him. It wasn't hard to see that Ulbrich valued a good position far more than anything he might be able to gain through blackmail.

Did Welker not care that a clueless Karl-Heinz Ulbrich was taking over from the very efficient Vera Soboda? Was that what Welker wanted? Did she know too much about what was going on? But how could he know how much she knew? Had the tracking device recorded her escapades in the system? If he knew this and had intentionally replaced her with the clueless Ulbrich so he could continue laundering money, then what did this tell me about Schuler's death?

6

Dirty work

Vera Soboda had barely greeted me when the doorbell rang.

"You thought you'd scared me off!" Karl-Heinz Ulbrich said to me triumphantly. "You thought that's why I let you go, right? I just wanted to see who was helping you." He looked at Vera. "You'll regret this. If you think that the Sorbian bank will give you your severance pay while you double-cross us, you've got another thing coming."

She glared at him as if she were about to grab him by the neck. If I had thrown myself between them, not much would be left of either him or me. Her eyes pinned on him, she asked me: "Did you find out anything?"

"No. And yet I see why Welker would have replaced you with him. You know what's going on, he doesn't. And yet that still doesn't prove a thing."

"What is it that I don't know?" Ulbrich asked.

"Ignorant idiot!" she said, full of disgust. "I'd get off my high horse if I were you! Why do you think Welker made you the new bank manager, when you know as much about banking as I know about ostrich farming? Do you think it's because you're able to run the bank? Nonsense! The only reason you've been hired is because there's no way you'll ever find out that money is being laundered at the bank. Though that isn't the only reason you were hired: it was also because of the way you handle the employees, and the fact that you wouldn't shrink back from any sort of nastiness."

"How dare you! It's not as if banking is some hocus-pocus. And whatever I need to know, I find out right away. Would I have caught the two of you otherwise? I used to be at the Head Office 18, National Security, where they hired only the best. The best! Money laundering! Don't make me laugh."

"You were with the Stasi?" Vera said, looking at him first in astonishment and then as if she hadn't seen him in a long time and now was recognizing him feature by feature. "Of course. Once in the shit, always in the shit. If no longer for our side, then for the other side. Whoever happens to need you guys and will pay you."

"Shit? This man entered the bank illegally, and you are making terrible and unsubstantiated allegations. That's shit! And what do you mean, I'm not working for our side but the other side? How could I work for our side? You're talking as if I had betrayed our side—I haven't heard such nonsense in years! Our side no longer exists! The only thing that exists now is the other side!"

He was still trying to present himself in a superior way, but he sounded exhausted and desperate. As if he had believed in East Germany and the Stasi and loved his job and was lost without it. As if he were orphaned.

But Vera Soboda did not let go: in the old days he'd been with the Stasi, and now he was with a shady West German bank, ignorant when it came to banking, nasty to the bank employees, being saddled on her and then replacing her—she was too furious to notice his exhaustion and desperation and to take pity on him. Perhaps that was also too much to ask. "I know our side no longer exists, and I'm not accusing you of betrayal," she went on, "but what you did in the past was dirty work, and it's dirty work you're doing now. You're already preparing the firings, aren't you? Everyone knows that. Do you know what they're calling you at the bank? The angel of death! And don't get on your high horse just because everyone's afraid of you. One can also be frightened of a little toad if it's poisonous and disgusting enough."

"Frau Soboda," I intervened in an attempt to calm her down. But now Ulbrich could no longer hold back.

"*You* need to get off your high horse! If money was being laundered in the bank, it wasn't going on just in the past few weeks, but all the time you were there, with your knowledge, under your very nose! Did you do anything about it? Did you go to the police?" He looked triumphant again. "Shit? You were standing in it with both feet, and if you had your way, you'd be happy to still be standing in it. If anyone here is ready for any kind of nastiness, it's you!"

Now Vera Soboda looked exhausted. She shrugged her shoulders, raised her arms and then lowered them, and went from the hall where we were standing into the living room and sat down.

Ulbrich followed her, saying, "You're not getting out of this so easily. The least I expect is an apology." Then Ulbrich didn't know what else to say.

I went to the kitchen, got three beers from the refrigerator, opened them, and took them to the living room. I put one on the table in front of Vera Soboda, and one in front of an empty chair, and I sat down with one of the beers on the sofa. Ulbrich went over to the empty chair, stood next to it for a moment, and sat down carefully on its edge. He took the beer and slowly rolled it between his palms. It was so quiet that I could hear the computer humming lightly in the covered veranda.

"Cheers," Ulbrich said. He raised his bottle and drank. Vera looked at him and at me as if it had slipped her mind that we were there. Ulbrich cleared his throat. "I am sorry I fired you. It was nothing personal. I wasn't given a reason; I was just ordered to—there was nothing I could do. I'm also fully aware that I know nothing about banking. But perhaps the job doesn't require someone who knows the business. Perhaps all it needs is someone who can use the phone. I make a call when there's something I don't know and am told what to do." He cleared his throat again. "And as for what you said about doing dirty work for the other side, we don't have any say anymore—you don't and I don't—and whoever has nothing to say has to accept the job he's given. Nothing personal there, either." He took a long sip, burped quietly, wiped his mouth with the back of his hand, and got up. "Thank you very much for the beer. Good night."

7

Fried potatoes

"Has he gone?" Vera asked.

Ulbrich had pulled the door shut behind him so quietly, and gone down the stairs so softly, that no sound disturbed the silence.

"Yes," I replied.

"I behaved rather badly. And when I got a chance to make up for it, I ruined that, too. He was right, and he even tried to be nice. I was so angry I didn't even manage to say good night."

"Angry at him?"

"At him, at me, at his being so disgusting."

"He isn't disgusting."

"I know. I'm angry about that, too. In fact, I owe him an apology."

"Are the cold cuts in the refrigerator for us?"

"Yes. I was thinking of making some fried potatoes, too."

"I'll see to dinner," I said.

I found some boiled potatoes, onions, bacon, and oil. The chopping, the hissing in the pan, and the aroma did me good after the argument between Vera and Ulbrich. I have come to believe that setbacks don't make you a better person, just a smaller one. The setbacks in my life didn't make me better, and Vera Soboda and Karl-Heinz Ulbrich, too, had become smaller through the setbacks that came with Germany's unification and postunification. Setbacks don't cost you only what you have invested—every time, they cut away a piece of your belief that you will survive the next trial, the next battle, that you will manage to tackle your life.

I served the food and we ate. Vera wanted to know what had happened at the Sorbian bank, and I told her. I explained where I knew Ulbrich from and why I was certain he knew nothing of former or present money laundering at the bank. "He suspected that something crooked was going on at Weller and Welker, had talked about the Russian or Chechen Mafia, and might have been thinking of money laundering. But as for anything specific—he himself can't have found out anything, and I'm certain Welker wouldn't have clued him in. That is, if there's still anything to be clued into."

"I . . . I see I was quick to jump to conclusions," Vera said.

"Yes, you might have been."

"In that case," she said, "Ulbrich might be right in saying that the bank doesn't need a manager who knows anything about banking. Perhaps the Sorbian bank needs to economize because no more money is being laundered, and firings are called for, and they took the first step with me. Perhaps they wanted to get rid of me so I wouldn't make trouble with the other firings." She looked at me with a sad smile and shook her head. "That's just a fantasy; I wouldn't have made any trouble about the other firings."

I got up and took the trash bag with Schuler's money out of my suitcase. I told her how I'd gotten the money and how Schuler had probably stumbled upon it.

"There's a whole lot that needs to be done around here," I said. "Take the money and get it all done."

"Me?"

"Yes, you. I'm not saying you can do everything that needs doing. Just some of it."

"I . . . this is . . . This is quite a surprise. I don't know if I can . . . I mean, I do have some ideas. But you've seen how angry I can get, and when I get angry I really do foolish things. Wouldn't you want to approach someone who . . . well, someone who's better? How about you yourself?"

The following morning I found her in her nightgown in the kitchen. She had apportioned most of the money into little bundles on the table and was counting the rest with unparalleled dexterity.

"We were made to practice counting money the old way," she said with a laugh, "and whoever counted fastest was made supervisor."

"So you *are* taking up my offer?" I asked.

"There are almost a hundred thousand marks here. I'll account for every penny."

She handed me a little gray booklet. "I found it among the bills."

It was a passport from the Third Reich. I opened it and found a picture and the name Ursula Sara Brock, born October 10, 1911. A cursive *J* was stamped over it. It was clear that when it came to the money Schuler had left me a bequest. But why had he left me this passport? I leafed through it, turning it this way and that, and put it in my pocket.

8

Keep an eye out!

On the way back I took the autobahn. I wanted to float along in the stream of cars without distractions, without having to pay too much attention to the road. I wanted to think.

Who was Ursula Brock? If she were still alive she would be an old lady and could hardly have frightened Schuler to death. Would Samarin or his people have frightened him to death? Among the many unanswered questions was why they wouldn't have taken the money from him right away. Would Welker, who only later laundered money, if he was laundering money at all ... No, even if I could prove that Welker was laundering money now, it wouldn't make sense that he would have frightened Schuler to death. Unless, that is, he already knew he was going to inherit Samarin's money-laundering enterprise and was afraid of Schuler's insatiable inquisitiveness.

I drove in the right lane, among trucks, elderly couples in old Fords and Opels, Poles in rattling, smoking wrecks, and die-hard communists in Trabants. When an exhaust pipe in front of me stank too much I switched to the left lane and drove past the trucks, Poles, and communists until I found an elderly couple behind whom I pulled in again. In one car a plastic dog was enthroned in the back window, shaking his head from side to side and up and down with insight and sorrow.

What did I have to go on? A dark Saab on the Schlossplatz in Schwetzingen and Vera Soboda's replacement by Karl-Heinz Ulbrich—at the end of the day, this was so little that I asked myself if I really had any proof against Welker. Was I envious of his wealth, his bank, his house, his children? The ease with which he had achieved everything? The ease with which he sauntered through life? The ability to remain untouched by both the evil that befell him and the evil he wrought? Was it a case of age envying youth, the war and postwar generation envying the generation of the economic miracle, the guilty envying the innocent? Was I being gnawed at by his having shot Samarin and having put Nägelsbach in danger without batting an eye? Was it that I didn't feel so innocent and uninvolved?

I spent the night in Nuremberg. The following morning I set out early and was in Schwetzingen by eleven. Until seven I sat around in various cafés, keeping my eye on the bank. A few cars, a few clients on foot, a few employees who sat down on a bench on the square at lunchtime and who at six said their good-byes in front of the gate—that was all.

As I sat in my office that evening, Brigitte called and asked if my trip had been a success. Then she asked: "Does this mean your case has come to an end?"

"Almost."

While I was jotting down what I knew and didn't know, what still had to be done and still might be done, there was a knock at the door. It was Georg.

"I happened to be walking by and saw you at your desk," he said. "Do you have a moment?"

He had been riding his bike and now cleaned his glasses. Then he sat down opposite me in the cone of the desk lamp. He eyed the half-empty wine bottle. "You're drinking too much, Uncle Gerhard."

I poured myself another glass and made him some tea.

"There must be a file at the Restitution Office," he said. "The nephew's son who emigrated to London and died there in the 1950s must have put in a claim after the war for the restitution of the family fortune. The Nazis wrecked and ravaged his home so completely that his parents killed themselves. Maybe the son knew something and mentioned it."

I needed a few moments to see where he was heading. "You're talking about the silent partnership? Nobody here's interested in that anymore. Nobody was ever really interested in it; my client wasn't, and I wasn't. It was just that it took me a long time to realize what it was a pretext for."

But Georg was on a roll. "I looked further into the matter. In the fifties, restitutions were a big thing, and there was one case after another. Lots of minor cases, but also really major ones. Jews who'd been forced to sell factories, department stores, or land for next to nothing, who either wanted their property back or compensation. Don't you remember all that?"

Of course I remembered. Particularly the expropriations of Jews. There had been a naive Jew who didn't want to sell, and when his business partner extorted him he turned to the public prosecutor's office. When I started as a public prosecutor in 1942, this incident already lay some time back but still made for a good joke.

"Aren't you interested in what happened?" Georg asked.

"Why would I be?"

"Why would *you* be? I want to know," Georg said, staring at me obstinately. "I've tracked down the silent partner. I know what kind of guy he was. He was conservative and liked to listen to music, drink wine, and smoke Havanas. He'd been awarded a pile of medals, made a fortune providing expert legal advice to the nobility, and was a modest man who invested all his money for his niece and nephew. As far as I'm concerned he's alive and kicking."

"Georg—"

"He's dead, I know. It's just a way of putting it. But I find Laban interesting enough to want to know everything. What are you paying me, by the way, for the research I've done up to now?"

"I was thinking a thousand plus expenses. Speaking of which . . ." I wrote him a check for two thousand marks.

"Thanks. That'll be enough for me to get to Berlin and dig through the files. I've still got a few days until my job begins. I'll let you know what I find out."

"Georg?"

"Yes?"

I looked at his slim face, his serious, alert eyes, his lips that were usually lightly parted as if he were surprised.

"Keep an eye out for those skinheads."

He laughed. "I will, Uncle Gerhard."

"Don't laugh. And keep an eye out for those other guys, too!"

"I will."

He got up, still laughing, and left.

9

Blackouts

On Monday I called Philipp, but he didn't want to phone Dr. Armbrust on the doctor's first day back from vacation.

"You can't imagine how hectic things are here," he told me. "Give me till tomorrow, or better, Wednesday."

On Wednesday he dropped by my office.

"As I don't have much to report," he said, "the least I could do was come and tell you in person. This Doctor Armbrust is a very nice fellow. It turns out he's referred several patients to me over the years."

"Well?"

"I asked him if Schuler had asthma or any allergies. The answer was no. The only things wrong with Schuler were his high blood pressure and heart problems. He was taking Ximovan for insomnia, which doesn't make you drowsy the next day. He was taking an ACE inhibitor, Zentramin for his heart, and a diuretic. He was on Catapresan for blood pressure, a great medication as long as you don't stop taking it abruptly—if you do, you run the risk of blackouts."

I recognized the medications. They were among those I'd taken from Schuler's bathroom so Philipp could tell me about Schuler's possible condition. I had even started reading the package inserts. "Blackouts?"

"While driving, talking, doing anything that involves concentration," Philip said. "That's why we don't prescribe it to people who are scatterbrained, confused, or forgetful. Armbrust described Schuler as a somewhat odorous but exceptionally alert elderly gentleman."

"That was my impression, too."

"That's not to say that he might not have forgotten to take his pills. On the first day you stop, things are still fine. On the second day, too. But on the third day, significant blackouts can occur. Think of it in these terms: on day one and day two he wouldn't have felt all that well, thinking it might be the weather or the extra glass of beer he'd had the night before, or just that he was having a bad day, the way one sometimes does. On the third day, he wouldn't have been in a state to think a lot."

"Do you think that's what happened?"

"What?"

"That someone who takes a medication year after year might suddenly forget to take it."

Philipp threw up his hands. "If there's anything you learn as a doctor, it's that patients come in all shapes and sizes. Perhaps Schuler had had enough of his medications, or he'd been feeling so well taking them all that time that he felt he didn't need them anymore, or he took the wrong pills by mistake."

"Or none of the above."

"Sorry, but that's the way it is. Maybe Schuler took his pills day in and day out and simply drank too much beer in the evening. Don't start going after false leads, Gerhard! And take care of your heart!"

10

Old poop

Then Georg came back from Berlin. He had managed to keep out of the way of the skinheads, and of the others, too. And he had found the restitution file of Laban's nephew.

"Putting in a claim for restitution was almost as painful as losing the things one was putting in for," Georg said. "Two silver candelabras, twelve silver knives, forks, soup and dessert spoons, twelve soup plates and twelve dinner plates, a sideboard, a leather sofa and armchairs; estimated value, date of purchase, length of use, receipts or other documents of proof of ownership, witness statements, explanations as to why the estimates are being furnished in this manner, why the property was relinquished, are there witnesses that the apartment was ransacked during Kristallnacht, were the losses reported to the police, to the insurance company— perhaps there was no other way, but this was terrible. And yet Laban's nephew seemed to have done rather well in London. He had a place in Hampstead and a gallery that still exists and has a good name."

We were again sitting in my office, across from each other. Georg's face was beaming with enthusiasm. He was proud of what he had discovered and wanted to stay the course, find out more, find out everything.

"What more can there be to know?" I said.

He looked at me as if I had asked a foolish question. "Things like where he got the money to live in London in style, what happened to his sister, what happened to his great-uncle's estate? There was once a bust of Laban at the university in Strasbourg, which a professor I spoke with there is also trying to locate—imagine if I should come across it in a junk store in Strasbourg or somewhere in Alsace. One thing's for sure: I know where I'm going for my next vacation."

I, too, knew where I had to go. It was raining as I drove to Emmertsgrund, but by the time I got there the wind had swept the clouds from the sky and the sun was shining. The view to the west was very clear, and I spotted the nuclear power plant in Philippsburg, the towers of the Speyer Cathedral, the telecommunications tower in the Luisenpark, and the Collini-Center—everything looking as if it had been painted with a fine brush. While I was gazing at the landscape the clouds were piling up over the mountains of the Haardt, preparing the next rain.

Old Herr Weller sat in the same chair by the same window,

as if he hadn't moved an inch since my last visit. When I sat down he leaned forward until his nose was close to mine, his weak eyes scrutinizing my face. "You're not a young man. You're an old poop like me."

"The term is *old pop*."

"What did you really want when you came by last time?"

I laid the fifty marks that he had given me for the war grave on the table.

"Your son-in-law hired me to ascertain the identity of the silent partner who brought half a million to your bank around the turn of the century."

"You didn't ask me about that."

"Would you have told me?"

He didn't shake his head, nor did he nod. "Why didn't you ask me?"

I could hardly tell him that by that time my investigations had been not for but against his son-in-law. "It was enough for me to find out if your generation of Weller and Welker could really have simply forgotten a silent partner."

"And?"

"I never met Welker's father."

He laughed, bleating like a goat. "You can bet your life he never forgot anything!"

"Nor have you, Herr Weller. Why did you keep it a secret?"

"Secret, secret . . . Did you finish my son-in-law's case?"

"It was Paul Laban, a professor in Strasbourg, the most famous and sought-after specialist of his day, childless, but solicitous for his niece and nephew and their children. It doesn't look as if any of them enjoyed the legacy of his silent partnership." I waited, but he waited, too. "Furthermore, it wasn't the right time for Jews to enjoy their wealth in Germany."

"You're right about that."

"Sometimes it was better to get a little something and make it abroad than to lose everything," I added.

"Why are we old poops beating about the bush?" Herr Weller said. "The nephew's son emigrated to England and wasn't able to take anything out of Germany, so we saw to it that our London connections made sure he didn't have to start up there empty-handed."

"That must have cost the nephew a pretty penny."

"The only thing that's free is death."

I nodded. "So in your archives there must be a document from 1937 or 1938 in which the nephew relinquishes all rights and claims to the silent partnership. I can understand your preferring to keep that under wraps."

"I'm sure an old poop like you can understand. But today everyone likes dragging things like that out into the light and making a big song and dance about it. Because they don't understand how things were back then."

"Not that it's easy to understand."

He grew increasingly animated. "Not easy to understand? It wasn't nice, it wasn't pleasant! But what is so hard to understand about the old game, one side having what the other side wants? It's the game of games. It's what keeps finance, the economy, and politics going."

"But—"

"But me no buts!" He banged his hand down on the armrest. "See to your business and let others see to theirs. A bank has to keep its money together."

"Did the nephew's son get in touch after the war?"

"With us?"

I didn't answer, but waited.

"He stayed in London after the war."

I continued to wait.

"He refused to set foot on German soil ever again."

I continued waiting, and he laughed.

"What a hardheaded old poop you are!" he said.

I'd had enough of him. "The expression isn't *old poop*, it's *old pop*!"

"Ha!" Again he banged his hand down on the armrest. "Wouldn't you love it if things were still popping for you? But they're not! You should at least be happy you can still poop." He laughed his bleating goat's laugh.

"And?"

"His lawyer made it clear to him that he wouldn't get anything out of us. The inflation after World War I, Black Friday, the currency reform after World War II—even the biggest pile can be reduced to a few mouse droppings. And it's not as if he hadn't been well provided for. Not to mention the danger we exposed ourselves to; we could have ended up in a concentration camp."

"Was that his German lawyer?"

He nodded and said casually, "Yes, back then we Germans still held together."

11

Remorse?

Yes, that's how they were. For them the Third Reich, war, defeat, rebuilding, and the economic miracle were simply different circumstances under which they could conduct the same business: multiplying the money they owned or managed. It was true when they said that they hadn't been Nazis, that they had nothing against Jews, that they had stood firmly on constitutional ground. Everything for them was ground on which they stood and which made their enterprises bigger, richer, and more powerful. And yet they did this with the feeling that nothing else mattered. What good were governments, systems, ideas, people's happiness or pain if the economy wasn't flourishing? When there was no work and no bread?

Korten had been like that. Korten, my friend, brother-in-law, and enemy. That was how he had devoted himself to the Rhineland Chemical Works during the war and how after the war he had turned it into what it is today. For Korten, as for so many others, power and the success of the enterprise had become synonymous with his own power and success. What he took out of the enterprise for himself, he took with the certainty that he was serving what was vital: the Rhineland Chemical Works, the economy, the people. Until he fell from a cliff in Trefeuntec. Until I pushed him off that cliff.

I never regretted it. There have been times when I thought I ought to, because it was neither legally nor morally correct. But remorse never set in. Perhaps the other, older, harder morals that existed before those of today still prevail in our hearts.

It is only in one's dreams that an unmastered, unmasterable remnant remains. That night I dreamed that Korten and I were having an elegant meal at a table beneath a large old tree with overhanging branches. I don't remember what we talked about. It was a casual, friendly conversation. I enjoyed it because I knew we couldn't really expect to chat so warmly and easily after what had happened at Trefeuntec. Then I noticed how gloomy it was. At first I thought it was the dense foliage, but then I saw that the sky was stormy and dark, and I heard the wind rustling through the leaves. We talked as if everything was fine until the wind started tearing at us, ripping away the tablecloth along with the plates and glasses, finally carrying off Korten on the chair on which he was sitting: a mighty, enthroned Korten, his deep laughter echoing. I ran after him, trying to catch him, ran with outstretched arms, ran without the slightest hope of grabbing hold of him or his chair, ran so fast that my feet barely touched the ground. As I ran, Korten went on laughing. I knew he was laughing at me, but I didn't know why, until I noticed that I had run beyond the edge of the cliff on which we had been sitting beneath the tree, that I was running on air, the sea far below me. My running came to an end, and I fell.

12

Summer

Suddenly summer was here: not just the odd warm day or mild evening, but a heat as oppressive in the shade as in the sun, a heat that didn't let me sleep at night but made me count the hours struck by the bell of the Heilig-Geist church. I was relieved when it grew light, though I knew that the morning was not fresh and the new day would turn out as hot as the day before. I got up and had some of the tea I'd made the night before and put in the refrigerator. Sometimes the scrapes and wounds that Turbo brought back from his nightly adventures were so bad that I had to tend them with iodine. He, too, is growing old. I wonder, does he still win his battles?

It was so hot that everything was less important, less pressing. As if it were not really true, just possible. As if one first had to find out what it was all about, and for that it was too hot.

But I don't want to blame the heat. I didn't know what else I could still do to shed light on Schuler's death. Perhaps there wasn't anything to shed light on and never had been. Had I taken a wrong turn? In a sense, this idea had its good side. If he had been attacked, it wasn't as if I'd have been any less responsible than I first thought. Just the opposite, in fact. Only if Schuler's bad condition had been triggered by someone else on that fatal day, would his life have been in my hands. In fact, if he only had a hangover, or had been affected by the weather, his accident could have occurred at any time.

The hot weeks ended with a series of days in which the heat exploded in powerful evening storms. By five o'clock the sky would cloud over, and by six it was as dark as if nighttime had come. The wind rose and whipped the dust through the streets, ripping from the trees branches that the heat had turned dry and brittle. With the first storms the children remained outside, yelping beneath the raindrops, overjoyed when the rain started pouring down like a waterfall, wetting them through and through. But this soon bored them. I sat by the door of my office and watched the water washing in waves over the empty sidewalk, gurgling in a pool over the gutter because the drain couldn't handle it fast enough. When the storm was over I was the first to go outside, breathing in the fresh air on my way home or to Brigitte's. During the storm the sun had set. But the sky was clear again, a pale blue glowing violet in the twilight before it turned a darker violet, dark blue, dark gray, black.

I savored the summer. I savored the heat and the law of lassitude with which it blanketed everything and beneath which I felt free and at ease. I savored the storms, and also the moderate temperatures of the following weeks. Brigitte and I were looking for an apartment, and when I insisted on one with a view of the Rhine or the Neckar she knew that I wasn't out to sabotage our search. I always would have liked to have a house by the sea, or if not by the sea then by a lake. But Mannheim isn't by the sea or by a lake. The Rhine and Neckar flow through it.

"We'll find a really good apartment, Gerhard."

Everything was fine but not fine. The stories life writes demand endings, and as long as a story doesn't have an ending, it keeps everyone who participates in it in check. It doesn't have to be a happy ending. The good don't have to be rewarded and the bad punished. But the threads of fate cannot be left dangling: they have to be woven into the story's tapestry. Only when that is done can we leave the story behind us. Only then are we free to begin something new.

No, the story that had started at the beginning of the year in the snow was not yet over. Even if I'd have liked to make peace with Schuler, who'd maybe had one glass too many or been affected by the weather. I didn't know all the threads that were still waiting to be woven into the carpet, and I knew even less what the carpet's pattern was or how I could find out. But all I had to do was wait. Stories strive toward their ends, and don't leave you alone until they reach them.

13

Laban's children

When the leaves began to turn I got a letter from Georg. He sent me a manuscript that was scheduled to be published in a law journal. "Laban's children"—Georg had turned his research on Laban's heirs into an article. Did I have any suggestions?

He made it clear from the start of the article that Laban did not in fact have any children. No natural children, and no disciples, either. While other professors guard their circle of students like mother hens, Laban saw to it that his students would stand on their own feet as soon as possible and follow their own paths. Georg suspected that an early passion for a colleague's wife, one that was perhaps reciprocated but that remained unfulfilled, had marked him in a way that kept him from close bonds with students and from deep relationships with women.

But he *did* have children. He was as close to his sister's two children as he might have been had they been his own. He particularly favored his nephew, Walter Brock, who had also become a lawyer and judge.

Walter Brock. Georg described his path from Breslau to Leipzig, his career from district court judge to judge of the regional high court, the insults, the humiliations, and finally the firing with which his career came to an end in 1933. He described his marriage; his children, Heinrich and Ursula; his and his wife's suicides after their apartment was ransacked during Kristallnacht. He described how Heinrich had escaped to London at the eleventh hour, and how Ursula hadn't managed to get out in time and so had gone into hiding when the deportations began. She had disappeared. Laban, who died in 1918, had tenderly loved little Ursula, who was born in 1911.

There was no need for me to double-check, but I took Ursula Brock's passport out of my filing cabinet and saw that her date of birth was October 10, 1911. Then I studied her passport photograph. She had had bobbed dark hair and a dimple in her left cheek, and she looked at me attentively with happy, somewhat startled eyes.

I found Georg at the courthouse. "I've got Ursula Brock's passport."

"You've got what?"

"Ursula Brock, Laban's great-niece. I've got her passport. I just read your article, and—"

"I've got a case at two. Can I drop by afterward?"

"Sure, I'll be at the office."

He came by and wouldn't take coffee, tea, or mineral water.

"Where is it?"

He studied the initial pages with the photograph and the entries and leafed through the rest of the pages slowly and carefully, as if he might be able to elicit hidden information from them.

"Where did you get this?" he asked.

I told him about Adolf Schuler, his archive, and his visit. "He gave me an attaché case that had . . . that had this passport in it—after which he got into his car, drove off, crashed into a tree, and died."

"This means that after she went into hiding she sought help in Schwetzingen. Did she find help? Did Weller and Welker get her a new passport? Did they keep this old one for after the war?" He shook his head slowly and sadly. "But she didn't make it."

"In your article you wrote that as a Jew she was expelled from the university in 1936. Do you know what she studied?"

"All kinds of things. Her parents were very indulgent and didn't push her. In the end it was Slavonic studies." He looked at me entreatingly. "Do you need the passport? Can I have it? I've got a picture of Walter Brock and his wife with the small children, and one of Heinrich in London, but I haven't got a picture of Ursula as an adult."

He took an envelope out of his briefcase and laid out a series of photographs on my desk. A married couple standing in front of a carefully pruned hedge, the man wearing a suit with a stiff collar beneath his chin and a walking stick in his left hand, the woman in a long dress down to the ground, with a strap in her right hand that harnessed Heinrich around shoulders and chest, like a horse's bridle. Heinrich was wearing a sailor suit and cap, and Ursula, bigger than her brother and not in a harness, was standing next to her father. She was wearing a summer dress and a wide sun hat. "Don't move," the photographer had just called out, and they all were standing still, unblinking. Another picture showed a young man in front of the Tower Bridge, which had just been raised to let a ship pass through.

"Heinrich in London?" I asked.

Georg nodded.

"And this is the house in Breslau in which Laban was born, this is his villa in Strasbourg, this is a postcard of the main building of the Wilhelm University under construction, and—"

"Who's that?" I asked, pulling out a photograph from beneath the postcards. I recognized the large head, the receding hairline, the large ears, and the protruding eyes. I had seen him the first time through a foggy windshield on the Hirschhorner Höhe and for the last time quite close up when we drove from the hospital to the Luisenpark. I had also seen him when we got out of the car and walked into the park. But Samarin's head had never made as much of an impression on me as when we sat next to each other on the backseat; he looking stoically before him while I peered at him from the side.

"That's Laban. Haven't you seen him before?"

14

Zentramin

So I drove yet again to the retirement home in Emmertsgrund. The first yellow and red leaves were glowing in the green of the mountains. In some of the fields fires were burning, and at one point the fire stretched all the way to the autobahn. I opened the window to see if it still smelled the way it used to, but only wind came roaring through the open window.

The door to old Herr Weller's apartment stood open, and the place had been emptied. I went inside and looked out the window at the cement factory from the spot where he and I had sat across from each other and talked. Two cleaning ladies came in and began to mop the floor without paying any attention to me. I wondered why the walls weren't being painted first. When I asked them what had happened to Weller, they didn't understand.

In the main office I was told that he had died of a stroke the week before. I've never been interested in medicine, nor will I ever be. I imagined old Herr Weller's brain at work, driven, sly, evil, propelled by bleating laughter like a stuttering engine. Until the engine suddenly stalled. I was told when and where he would be buried. I could still make it if I hurried. I suddenly remembered Adolf Schuler's funeral. It had slipped my mind, and again I felt as if I'd failed to hold on to him and stop him from getting into the car and driving into a tree.

Old Herr Weller had enjoyed talking to me and would have wanted to talk more—to explain how things were during the war, that the great-niece of his silent partner would have died if he and old Herr Welker hadn't taken her in and given her a new identity; that she'd been insane to have a damn brat on top of everything, as he'd have put it. That he and Welker had done more than enough, raising the brat after she died. The brat's real identity? What use would that have been to Gregor Samarin if they'd informed him of his real identity? That would just have given him big ideas. Furthermore, the Brocks lived in Leipzig. Wouldn't the brat have had a better time of it as Gregor Samarin in the West than he would growing up in a Communist orphanage?

Yes, that's how old Herr Weller would have spoken to me, one old poop to another. I could picture it clearly. Had I asked him whether a Gregor Brock wouldn't have a right to claims that a Gregor Samarin couldn't make because he didn't know anything about them, old Herr Weller would have waved me away. Claims? What claims? After the inflation, the Great Depression, and the currency reform? Claims, when he himself and old Herr Welker could have been sent to a concentration camp for all they had done for Ursula Brock?

I could also picture a conversation that would have taken place in the spring between Adolf Schuler and Bertram Welker. Schuler would have been waiting for Welker to fill him in about Samarin, about his identity and his dealings. Schuler had found the money in the cellar, and in his search for documents concerning the silent partner had found the passport: the passport of Ursula Brock, whom he had known only as Frau Samarin. Perhaps he felt obliged to inform Samarin as well. But his foremost loyalty was to the Welkers, so he intended to go to Bertram Welker first with the information. But Welker had come with Samarin, and Schuler couldn't talk with Welker as openly as he would have liked. Schuler had been secretive, Welker had said, and probably he really had aired a few secrets, not so much about the money as about Gregor Brock. Also, perhaps it wasn't Welker but Samarin who had diarrhea and kept having to go to the bathroom. Perhaps Schuler was lucky and managed to tell Welker everything he wanted to tell him.

Or had that been Schuler's undoing?

I drove to my office and took out the medicines I had taken with me from Schuler's bathroom. I took the little bottle of Catapresan pills to the Kopernikus pharmacy, where the four friendly pharmacists have been so helpful and forthcoming over the years that I've almost never needed a doctor. I gave the bottle to the head pharmacist. She told me she wasn't sure when she'd have an answer for me. But when I dropped by my office that evening after a meal at the Kleiner Rosengarten, she had tested the contents and left the results on my answering machine. The pills were not Catapresan, but

Zentramin, a benign magnesium-calcium-potassium concoction used for calming the vegetative nervous system and stabilizing the cardiac nerves during arrhythmia. I knew this medication. Zentramin was also among the medications that Dr. Armbrust had prescribed for Schuler, and which I had found in his bathroom. Zentramin pills look remarkably similar to Catapresan pills.

15

Not to mention the language!

I hadn't yet had the opportunity to consider a plan of action. I was standing in my doorway getting the key out of my bag when I heard "Herr Self!" and Karl-Heinz Ulbrich stepped out of the shadows into the light of the door lamp. He was again wearing his three-piece suit, but his vest was unbuttoned, his collar undone, and his tie crooked. He had stopped trying to play the banker.

"What are you doing here?"

"Can I come in?" he asked. When I hesitated a moment, he smiled. "As I've told you once before, the lock on your door's a joke."

We climbed the stairs in silence. I unlocked the door and

had him sit on one of the sofas, as he had before, while I sat on the other. I felt I was being petty. I got up and brought out a bottle of Sancerre, along with two glasses.

"Would you like some wine?"

He nodded. Turbo came over and again rubbed against his feet.

"The mistakes we make," he suddenly began. "All the things we don't know! Of course one can always learn, but for us East Germans to have to learn at the age of fifty what you West Germans learned at twenty is difficult, and a mistake that doesn't affect a person at twenty can be very painful at fifty. Tax returns, insurance, bank accounts, the contracts you people keep signing about every single thing—we had no idea about any of that. Not to mention the language! I still can't tell when you people mean something or don't. It's not just when you're lying, but words have a whole other meaning when you present yourselves or are pitching or selling something."

"I can imagine that that's—"

"No, you can't. But it's kind of you to say so." He picked up a glass and drank. "When Welker offered me the job, I thought at first that you had warned him about me and that he was trying to buy me off. Then I thought: But why? Why do I always think along those lines? Welker and I had a good conversation. It didn't bother him that I had specialized in financial crimes or that I'd been with the Stasi or that I was from the East. He said he needed someone like me. I told myself that I wanted to believe what he was saying, that I also wanted to believe in myself, that banking wasn't just some hocus-pocus. I began reading the financial news, even if it's far from an easy read, and ordered some books about management and bookkeeping.

You know, it's not as if you people here in the West don't breathe the same air we do. And you don't even know the local people, while I know the Sorbians like the back of my hand."

I don't know what was wrong with me. I remembered the text and melody of a hit by Peter Alexander from the 1960s: "I know your sorrows like the back of my hand."

"I really tried hard," he continued, staring in front of him. "But once again I didn't understand the language. What Welker had in fact said—a thing you would have understood in a flash—was: 'I need an idiot who doesn't know what's going on here. And Karl-Heinz Ulbrich is just such an idiot.'"

"When did you realize this?"

"Oh, weeks ago. Quite by chance. We've got a lot of small branches in the area, and I thought I ought to get to know them, so I went to visit them—each time a different one. One day I turned up at one, in the back of beyond, just five little houses, all boarded up as if nobody lived there, on a road to nowhere. The bank itself was in no better shape, and I wondered what it was doing there. Well, what could it be doing there? It was a place to accommodate money. It didn't take me long to find that out. When I want to know something, I—"

"I know, when it comes to shadowing you're an absolute ace."

"I didn't just shadow. I also sniffed around. Welker isn't Mafia. His men are Russians and he works for Russians, that's all. Before his men started working for him, they worked for that other fellow, the one he shot. And he doesn't only work for Russians. He's independent, makes a profit of four to six percent, which isn't a lot, but then again that's all that laundering brings in. Where you make money is when you launder large amounts. Then you *really* take it in. And what Vera Soboda and I realized is that laundering cash is only an extra. The actual business is the laundering of money on the books."

"Did you go to the police?"

"No. If it all comes to light it will be the end of the Sorbian bank, and all my employees will be out on the street. I didn't have to read too much in my financial textbooks to see that we have far too many employees. The only reason Welker doesn't rock the boat is because he doesn't want to make waves. And do you know what else I tell myself? In the old days, we never had anything like that happen. You fellows brought all this with you. So it's *your* police who should be dealing with it."

"I can assure you that we in Schwetzingen had as little money laundering in the old days as you did in Cottbus. Wasn't it you who said that Chechens, Georgians, and Azer-baijanis—"

"Back in the East German days, the Chechens stayed in Chechnya and the Georgians in Georgia. It's you people who mixed everything up."

He had a fixed idea in his mind and would not let anyone shake it. There was a determined look on his face, even if his determination was one of inflexibility.

"So what now? Why are you here? From what I see, you've reconciled yourself to the fact that—"

"Reconciled myself?" He looked at me in disbelief. "You think that because I haven't gone to the police I have bowed my head to all the derision, insults, humiliations, degradations . . ." He groped for other fitting expressions but couldn't find any. "I intend to do something!"

"How long have you been in town?"

"A week. I took a leave of absence. I'll do something that Welker won't forget."

"Oh, Herr Ulbrich. I don't know what you have in mind, but won't the Sorbian bank be ruined that way, too, with your employees all ending up on the street? Welker wasn't out to deride or humiliate you, or any of the other things you just said. What he did was use you, just as he uses everyone else, regardless of whether they're from East or West Germany. It's nothing personal."

"He said to me—"

"But he doesn't speak your language. You yourself just said that you and we don't speak the same language."

He looked at me sadly, and with a shock I realized it was the same helpless, somewhat foolish look that Klara sometimes had. I also recognized Klara's inflexible determination in his face.

"Don't do anything, Herr Ulbrich. Go back and earn some money at the Sorbian bank for as long as you can—it isn't going to last forever. Earn enough so you can open an office, in Cottbus or Dresden or Leipzig: Karl-Heinz Ulbrich, Private Investigator. And if you're ever swamped with work, give me a call and I'll come help you out."

He smiled—a small, crooked smile despite his inflexible determination.

"Welker used you," I continued. "So now use him. Use him to lay a foundation for what you want to do. Don't get tangled up in settling scores where if you win, you'll end up the loser."

He was silent. Then he emptied his glass in a single draft.

"That's a good wine." He leaned forward and sat there as if he didn't know whether to remain sitting or get up.

"Why don't we finish this bottle?" I asked.

"I think . . ." He got up. "I think I'd better go. Thank you for everything."

16

A little joke

I finished the bottle on my own. So, Ulbrich wanted to do something that Welker wouldn't forget. If he had designs on Welker's life, he would have expressed himself differently. But what did he have in mind? And what could it be that Welker would never forget? Welker, who had such a knack for keeping the good things clear in his mind and forgetting the bad?

I thought about Schuler and Samarin. If Welker hadn't forgotten them yet, he would soon enough. What had happened to them, what he had done to them, was bad. What would Ulbrich do that Welker wouldn't forget? Kill him? The dead never forget.

I didn't sleep well. I dreamed of Korten falling off the cliff, his coat fluttering. I dreamed of our final conversation, of my saying, "I have come to kill you." And his mocking words: "To bring them back to life?" I dreamed of Schuler staggering toward me, and of Samarin in his straitjacket. Then everything got confused; Welker fell from the cliff, and Schuler said mockingly: "To bring me back to life?"

The following morning I called Welker. I had to talk to him.

"Are you planning an investment?" he asked cheerfully.

"I'm planning a deposit, an investment, a withdrawal—it depends on how you look at it."

Two new batteries, and my old voice recorder was working again. You can get smaller ones today that record better and longer and that look more elegant. But my old recorder did the job. My old corduroy jacket did the job, too. It has a hole behind the lapel and one in the breast of the jacket so that the wire, hidden from view, can pass from the recorder in the inside pocket to the microphone in the lapel. Whenever I take my handkerchief out of my inside pocket to wipe the sweat off my forehead or blow my nose, I can turn the recorder on or off.

At ten o'clock I was sitting in Welker's office.

"As you see," he said, his hand sweeping through the air, "nothing has changed since your last visit. I wanted to renovate the place, refurbish everything and make it all more attractive. But I just can't get to it."

I looked around. It was true that nothing had changed. Only the leaves of the chestnut trees I could see through the window had begun to turn.

"As you know," I said, "Herr Schuler came to see me before his Isetta crashed into the tree and he died. It wasn't only the money he brought me. He also brought me what he had found out about Laban and Samarin."

Welker didn't say anything.

"He told you what he had found the evening you and Samarin went to see him, when Samarin happened to step out for a moment."

Again Welker didn't say anything. He who says nothing says nothing wrong.

"Later, when you were outside, you saw that Schuler was taking a blood-pressure medication that one mustn't stop taking abruptly. You know a thing or two about such matters. Then you looked through Schuler's arsenal of medicines to find some pills that looked similar to his blood-pressure medication, and you found some. You switched the pills, just like that. Perhaps it would kill Schuler—which would be great. Perhaps it would only confuse him, indefinitely, for a long time, or perhaps just for a short period—not bad, either. Perhaps he would notice. But even then you wouldn't be taking a risk by switching the pills: Schuler would have blamed himself or his niece, but he never would have thought of suspecting you."

"Indeed," Welker said. He spoke the way one might when someone else is talking, and one wishes to indicate one is listening carefully and paying attention. He looked at me compassionately with his intelligent, sensitive, melancholic eyes, as if I had a problem and had come to him for help.

"I knew that you are also a doctor. But as long as I didn't understand your motive, I didn't make the connection between this fact and what I knew about the side effects of the blood-pressure medication and Schuler's condition before his accident. It was only then that I had the pills in the bottle checked."

"I see," he said. He didn't ask me: "What motive? What was my motive supposed to have been? Where do you see a motive?" All he said was "I see," and he continued sitting there quite at ease, looking at me compassionately.

"That was murder, Herr Welker, even if you weren't certain that switching the medicines would kill Schuler. Murder out of greed. Samarin's grandfather might have renounced all his rights and claims to the silent partnership in 1937 or 1938, but the action back then of a Jew in favor of an Aryan business partner isn't worth much. Samarin's claims would have become uncomfortable for you."

Welker smiled. "That would be quite ironic, wouldn't it, if the silent partnership, which was my pretext for bringing you into this affair, now posed a threat to me?"

"I don't think that's funny. I don't think your murder of Samarin is funny, either, a murder you committed with cold premeditation and which you presented to us as the act of a desperate man. I don't think it's funny that you're continuing Samarin's practices. No, I don't see anything comic in any of this."

"I said 'ironic', I didn't say 'comic.'"

"Ironic, comic—either way, I don't see anything I could laugh about. And when I weigh the fact that Samarin, who didn't murder Schuler, probably also didn't murder your wife—about which you always spoke with such emotion—then I stop laughing entirely. What happened to your wife? Did you find that she, having had a fatal accident, could be of some use as a murder victim? Or wasn't it an accident at all? Did you kill your wife?" I was furious.

I thought he would jump to his own defense. He had to. He couldn't allow me to get away with what I'd just said. But he uncrossed his legs, leaned his elbows on his knees, pursed his lips, sullen and sulking, and slowly shook his head. "Herr Self, Herr Self . . ."

I waited.

After a while he sat up in his chair and looked me straight in the eye. "It is a fact that Gregor, wearing a straitjacket, was shot in the Luisenpark. If you have something to say about how he came to be there, why he was in a straitjacket, and why he was killed, I suggest you go to the police. It is also a fact that Schuler had high blood pressure and that he drove into a tree in front of your office and died. If he came by to bring you something, if you were with him before the incident and saw that he was in a bad way, then why did you let him get into his car? From what I can see, there are one or two inconsistencies, if not more. Perhaps there are also one or two inconsistencies in the matter of my wife's death, where naturally the police suspected me first but ended up counting me out. We all have to learn to live with inconsistencies. We can't just start leveling unsubstantiated accusations . . ." He shook his head again.

I wanted to intervene, but he wouldn't let me.

"This is one of the things I wanted to tell you. The other is—how shall I put it?—I'm not interested in history: the Third Reich, the war, the Jews, silent partners, dead heirs, old claims! All that is water under the bridge. It has nothing to do with me, and I won't be drawn into it. It bores me. I also have no interest in East Germany. I'd be happiest if everyone in the East would just stay where they are. But when the East comes over here, strikes root, starts meddling and trying to take over my business, then I have to show them that that's not the name of the game. Samarin and his Russians came here to usurp me—don't forget that. The past, the past! I've had enough of it. Our parents bored us with all those tales of their suffering during the war, their deeds in rebuilding Germany, and their part in the economic miracle, the young teachers with their myths of 1968. Do you, too, have a tale to offer? Enough! My job is to keep Weller and Welker above water. We're an anachronism. On the great ocean of the world economy we're just a little barge among the oil tankers, container ships, destroyers, and aircraft carriers—a barge that gets tossed about in the rough seas through which all those other ships can sail smoothly. I don't know how long we can hold out. Perhaps my children won't be interested in continuing. Perhaps I myself will lose interest one day. As it is, I don't belong here. I'd have done better to become a doctor and collect art on the side or even to have picked up a brush myself. I'm old-fashioned, you know. Not in the sense that I'm in any way interested in the past. But I would have liked a quiet, old-fashioned kind of life. Old-fashioned—it's old-fashioned, too, that I followed family tradition and am now running the family bank. But the only way of doing this is all or nothing, and as long as I'm running this bank, as long as we Welkers still exist, nobody will take us for a sleigh ride." He repeated emphatically: "Nobody!" Then he smiled again. "I'm surprised you let me get away with that mixed metaphor. A barge can hardly be used for a sleigh ride."

He got up, and so did I. I'd had enough of his words—his well-considered, well-crafted lies, truths, and half-truths.

On the stairs he said: "It's amazing how old habits can come back to haunt one."

"What do you mean?"

"If Schuler hadn't made a habit of storing his Catapresan pills in those bottles, nobody could have replaced them."

"He didn't do it out of habit. His niece did it because with his arthritic fingers he couldn't get the pills out of the foil."

Then I remembered that though I had told him about a blood-pressure medication, I hadn't mentioned Catapresan. Had he just betrayed himself? I stopped.

He also stopped, turned to me, and looked at me pleasantly. "The medication *was* Catapresan, wasn't it?"

"I never . . ." But there was no point of capturing on tape: "I never mentioned the name of the medication." It wouldn't prove a thing. There was no point, either, in saying that to Welker. He knew it well enough. He had permitted himself a little joke.

17

Presumption of innocence

I went home and sat outside on the balcony. I smoked a cigarette, then another. The third tasted once again the way cigarettes used to when I smoked as many as I wanted.

I was furious. Furious at Welker, at his sense of superiority, his composure, his impudence. At how he'd gotten away with two murders, with the theft of the silent partnership, with money laundering. At how he'd let me know that he had done these things, all the while making it clear that I shouldn't presume to match myself against him. I shouldn't presume to match myself against *him*? *He* shouldn't presume he'd get away with this!

I called my friends and insisted they come over that

evening. The Nägelsbachs, Philipp, and Füruzan promised to be over by eight. "What are we celebrating?" "What's for dinner?" "Spaghetti carbonara, if you're hungry." Brigitte said she couldn't come till later.

They weren't hungry. They didn't know what to make of the sudden invitation and sat around expectantly, nursing their wine. All I told them was that I had spoken with Welker and had recorded the conversation. I played them the tape. When it ended, they looked at me questioningly.

"If you remember, Welker hired me to find the silent partner, just to bring me into the game without Samarin suspecting anything. Banks and family stories, stories of yesterday and the distant past—it all sounded innocent enough. Welker wanted me in the game so I'd be there when he got the opportunity to move against Samarin. The matter of the silent partner didn't interest him at all. But then the silent partner *did* become interesting. He took on a face—and not in a figurative sense, but a literal one. A face with a receding hairline, large ears, and protruding eyes. You'll recognize this face." I handed them Laban's picture.

"Well I'll be damned!" Philipp said.

"Old Herr Weller and Herr Welker had acted correctly enough: they helped the silent partner's great-nephew establish himself financially in London and saw to it that the great-niece, who hadn't managed to leave Germany in time, got new papers under the name Samarin. When she died, they looked after her child. Though as the boy was born with the name Gregor Samarin, they also raised him as such. The great-nephew died in London, and the great-niece had disappeared as 'Ursula Brock.' The silent partner's share was to go unclaimed for good."

"How big was this share?"

"I'm not exactly sure. When Laban brought his money into the bank, it was as much as the bank itself had. The bank had been on the brink of bankruptcy. I have no idea how from a bookkeeping standpoint his share might be valued up or down over the years."

"What part did Schuler play in all of this?"

"Schuler had been Welker's and Samarin's teacher, and later the bank's archivist. When I mentioned to him that Welker was interested in the silent partner and that I was to shed light on his identity, Schuler was gripped by jealousy. He wanted to prove that he was more capable than I, that he could look into all of that without me. He burrowed through the bank's archives until he got lucky. This is the passport of Laban's great-niece."

Frau Nägelsbach turned it this way and that.

"How did Schuler know that Ursula Brock was Laban's great-niece?" she asked. "And how did he conclude that she was Samarin's mother?"

"He had known her as Frau Samarin and Gregor's mother, and any documents concerning the Brocks could only have been in the silent partner's file. Along with this passport he might also well have found some other documents that he didn't give me. Not to mention that he found something else that he did bring me: money that was to be laundered at the bank. That money made me miss finding the passport for quite a while. What I initially thought was that Schuler had threatened Samarin with exposing his money-laundering racket and had consequently signed his own death warrant. But all the while, he had signed his death warrant by revealing to Welker that he knew Samarin's true identity. What Welker did then was to switch Schuler's pills. That wasn't a fail-safe way of killing him, but it was worth a try. If it succeeded, it would get Schuler out of the way; if it didn't, there was always time for a second attempt. Welker wasn't in a hurry. He knew how loyal Schuler was and that he wouldn't immediately go to Samarin with what he had found out. But it worked. Schuler was in a bad way, became disoriented, and drove into a tree. And yet Schuler was alarmed by fact that he was feeling worse and worse, so he quickly brought me what he had found: the money and the passport."

"Blood-pressure medication?" Herr Nägelsbach said. "I admit to being a hypochondriac, Reni is one, too, and I'm interested in medicine. But I had no idea you could kill a person with blood-pressure medication."

"You can't actually kill anyone with it," Philipp explained, "but if you're on Catapresan and suddenly stop taking it, you run the risk of blackouts. The only question is how Welker could have known . . ."

"He studied medicine," I said. "After he finished his studies, he sacrificed his medical career to the bank."

"What happened then?"

"You mean after Schuler's death? As you know, Welker shot Samarin, leading us to believe that he had been overwhelmed by pain, sorrow, and anger. But the truth is that he shot him with a cool hand and in cold blood. He wanted to get rid of Samarin, the silent partner's heir, the lackey who all of a sudden wanted a say in the bank, the man with dangerous connections who was blackmailing him, the man with the lucrative connections who was standing in his way."

They sat there in silence for a while.

"Why are you telling us all this?" Philipp asked.

"Don't you find it interesting?"

"It *is* interesting. But to be perfectly honest, it's the kind of thing I'd have preferred not to know," Philipp said. I must have looked at him as if he were mad. "Don't get me wrong, Gerhard. I'm a practical man. I'm interested in things you can do something about: operating on a heart, fixing my boat, cultivating my flowers, making Füruzan happy." He laid his hand on hers and looked at her so devotedly that everyone laughed. "But we simply can't not do anything!" Philipp continued. "We got involved, we helped Welker, we . . . Well, if it hadn't been for us, Samarin would still be alive!" I understood Philipp less and less. "Didn't you say that the world we thought was Samarin's world and which we now know to be Welker's, isn't your world and that you don't want to give up your world without a fight? Isn't any of that true anymore?"

"That was different," I replied. "Back then we thought Welker was in danger and wanted to help him. Who do you want to help now? Who's in danger? Nobody. And as for the world no longer being . . . Perhaps I went a little overboard. What I meant was about danger and helping."

Frau Nägelsbach eyed me quizzically. "Only a few weeks ago you were against—"

"No, I wasn't against informing the police. I only felt that your husband and Philipp both had to agree what they would do. The possible consequences were more serious for them than they'd have been for me."

Philipp shook his head. "My contract with the private hospital is as good as sealed. But what would happen if there were a scandal?"

"I'm afraid, Herr Self, that we missed the right moment, if there ever was one," Nägelsbach said. "Back then the lead was fresh and we were good witnesses. Today we're bad witnesses. Why did we keep silent for so long? Why are we speaking up now? Furthermore, it was dark, we didn't see Welker shoot Samarin, there were no prints on the murder weapon, and Welker will deny everything. As for Schuler's murder, things look even bleaker. A public prosecutor might make a case against Welker for money laundering, but it wouldn't be easy."

Nobody said anything, and in the silence I felt as if everyone was waiting for me to officially drop the subject, to leave them alone. But I couldn't. "We know Welker has two murders on his conscience. Doesn't that interest us? Don't we have some kind of obligation?"

Nägelsbach shook his head. "Haven't you heard of the presumption of innocence? If Welker can't be convicted, he can't be convicted. It's as simple as that."

"But we—"

"Us? We should have gone to the police right away. We didn't, and now it's too late. Do you remember what I told you when this happened? How can you think I would ever agree to our taking justice into our own hands?"

The silence in the room was oppressive until Philipp could no longer bear it. "Herr Nägelsbach—Rudi, if I'm not mistaken? Rudi, if I may call you that. Would you like to join Gerhard, me, and an old friend of ours in a game of Doppelkopf every two weeks, or perhaps even once a week?"

Nägelsbach was uncomfortable. He is a man of old-fashioned, formal politeness. He tends to recoil at overfamiliarity. Being addressed by his first name took him aback, and he was put out by the abrupt change of subject. But he made an effort. "Thank you, Philipp. That is very kind of you, and I would be delighted. But I do insist that when any of us holds the two aces of hearts—"

"That they will be the piglets." Philipp laughed.

"Gerhard?" Füruzan said, so solemnly that Philipp stopped laughing and the others sat up.

"Yes, Füruzan."

"I'll come with you. Perhaps I can lend a hand when you bump off Welker or set fire to his bank. As long as you don't do anything to his children, okay?"

18

Not God

Brigitte came at eleven. "Where are your friends? You didn't have a fight, did you?" She sat down on the arm of my chair and laid her hand on my shoulder.

"Yes and no."

We had parted amicably enough, but our conviviality had suffered a bump, and we had all been a little awkward when saying our good-byes. I told Brigitte what I had reported to my friends, what I had hoped for, and how they had reacted.

"Oh, Gerhard. I see their point and I also see yours, but they . . . Why don't you go to the police and at least get Welker on money laundering?"

"He's got two lives on his conscience."

"What about his wife?"

"We'll never know that for sure. Everything points to the fact that she really had an accident and that he wasn't the one who—"

"That's not what I meant. I'm quite aware that he ought to be convicted for murder. But there's not enough to convict him on. It's not as if he's the only criminal running around free when he ought to be in prison. Do you want to hunt them all down?"

"They're nothing to me, but Welker—"

"What's Welker to you? Tell me. Your paths crossed, and that was that. I'd understand if there'd at least been a personal connection between you."

"Quite the opposite: if there *was* something personal, then I really wouldn't have the right to . . ." I fell silent. Years ago, in Trefeuntec, I'd taken justice into my own hands. Was I now trying to prove to myself that I had done that on principle, and that I was not out to settle a personal score, either then or now?

Brigitte shook her head. "You're not God."

"No, Brigitte, I'm not God. I just can't come to terms with the fact that Welker killed Schuler and Samarin, that he's wealthy and content, and that's all there is to it."

She looked at me sadly, concerned. She took my head in her hands and kissed me on the lips. She held my head and said, "Manu is waiting for me; I've got to go. Forget Welker."

She saw in my eyes how my powerlessness was tormenting me.

"Is it so bad? Is it so bad because you think you're old if you don't do anything?" I didn't reply. She searched my eyes for an answer. "Forget Welker. Only if . . . only if it'll kill you if you don't do anything. But in that case be careful, do you hear? I don't give a damn about Welker, whether he's alive or dead, doing well or badly. But I do give a damn about you."

She left and I went out on the balcony and smoked, looking into the night. Yes, Brigitte was right. My powerlessness was tormenting me because my age made me feel it. It seared my memory how often I had realized after the fact that I'd been too slow. It seared my guilt at Schuler's death into my mind. It forever sealed that neither as a public prosecutor nor as a private detective had I left behind anything I could be truly proud of. It consumed me like a rage, a fear, a pain, an insult. I had to do something if I didn't want it to devour me entirely.

Before I went to bed I took from a drawer the revolver that had been there for years. I hadn't had a weapon for many years, and hadn't planned on having this one, either, but once I got this revolver I couldn't throw it away. A client had given it to me to look after and failed to retrieve it. I put it on the kitchen table and eyed it: black, handy, deadly. I picked it up, weighed it in my hand, and put it back on the table. Should I put it under my pillow to get closer to it?

19

With siren and flashing blue lights

It was still dark when I woke up, and I knew something was wrong. Something in my chest wasn't right and was filling the space in which I breathe and in which my heart expands when it beats. It wasn't a pain, but it was present: restricting, persistent, dangerous.

All of a sudden my forehead and palms were covered in sweat. I was frightened—I felt as if whatever wasn't right in my chest was fear, a tough, fluid, corroding mass of fear.

I got up, walked a few steps, opened the window and then the door to the balcony, and took a deep breath. But whatever wasn't right in my chest didn't go away. It grew. It turned into a pressure, and my fear turned into panic.

The pressure abated and I calmed down. Hadn't my last heart attack sent a numbness along my left arm? I felt nothing in my left arm. At that moment I decided that in the future I would live a healthier life, not smoke anymore, not drink anymore, and get some exercise. If Philipp went for the gold, couldn't I at least go for the bronze? I was immersed in pleasant and positive thoughts. Until the pressure returned and I again broke out in a sweat. I was gripped by panic when the pressure remained and increased, in a slow ebbing and flowing. I sat down on my bed, hugged my chest with both arms, rocked back and forth, and heard myself whimpering softly.

But the pressure had been only a forerunner of pain. It, too, came in waves, sometimes slow, sometimes fast: there was no regular rhythm I could count on. The first onslaught was like an electric shock that made my chest seize up. It electrified my brain, and with full clarity I realized I had to do something. If I didn't I would die. It was just after five in the morning.

I called the emergency service and twenty minutes later two paramedics from the Red Cross arrived with a stretcher—twenty minutes in which the pain cut through me like waves. Like labor pains—at least what I imagined labor pains to be—and whenever the pain kicked in, I took a deep breath. The paramedics made a few soothing remarks, got me onto the stretcher, and hooked me up to a drip from which a blood thinner flowed. They carried me down the five floors and put me in the ambulance. They turned on the flashing blue lights; through the window I could see them flaring over the wall of the building. Then they turned on the siren and drove off. They didn't drive fast. The drip and the plastic tube swung gently.

Was there also a tranquilizer in the drip? The pain didn't subside, but in its peaks and valleys my impressions became blurred and my fear disappeared into a whimpering resignation.

In the emergency room a lady doctor put stronger medications into my drip. These were supposed to dissolve the clot in my heart. I choked on gall and wondered why my gallbladder didn't like my thinning blood. The nurse didn't wonder; she reached for a kidney-shaped pan and held it under my chin.

After a while I was sent to intensive care. Corridor ceilings, swinging doors, elevators, doctors in green, nurses in white, patients and visitors. In a daze I took it all in, as if I were rolling on a silent train through a perplexing and seething swarm. At one point we went through a long corridor that was empty except for a patient in pajamas and dressing gown who followed me with his eyes, bored and without curiosity or pity. At times I managed to gag into the kidney-shaped pan that lay next to my head, at times I missed. It stank repulsively.

The pain had settled into my chest as if it had sized me up when it had first arrived in rising and ebbing waves and now knew that it was the sole proprietor. The pain had become even, an even pulling, a pulling into and out of my chest. After a few hours in intensive care it subsided, as did the vomiting. I was only exhausted, so exhausted that I thought it possible simply to fade out.

20

Crimes for lost honor

Philipp showed up in the afternoon and patiently explained to me what happens during an angiogram. Hadn't it already been explained to me once before? A catheter is inserted and pushed all the way up to the heart so that pictures can be taken: of your beating heart, of good arteries, constricted arteries, and blocked arteries. If luck isn't on your side the catheter irritates the heart, with the result that it can no longer maintain its rhythm. Or the catheter pries loose a thrombosis, which wanders off and blocks an artery at a vital point.

"Do I have a choice?"

Philipp shook his head.

"Then you don't need to explain all this."

"I thought you might find it interesting."

I nodded.

I also nodded when, after the angiogram, the surgeon informed me that two bypasses would be necessary. I didn't want to know why, how, or where. I didn't want to act to the doctors or nurses—and definitely not to myself—as if I had a say in any of this.

The surgeon told me of a colleague of his in Mosbach who'd had nine bypasses and then climbed the Katzenbuckel, the highest mountain of the Odenwald range. There was no need to worry; we'd just have to wait a few days until my heart had calmed down a little and was less vulnerable before we operated.

So I waited, and my exhaustion slowly began to fade. I was still tired. The fatigue allowed me to live down the loss of my autonomy, the tubes hooked to my wrist, the face that looked back at me in the mirror, and the fact that whenever I peed, half went astray. I dozed.

At times Brigitte sat by my bed, her hand resting on mine or on my forehead. She read to me but I got tired after a few pages. Or we would speak a few words, which I would often forget shortly afterward. I understood that Ulbrich was either still in Mannheim or that he had come back, and had been looking for me all over, and had finally found Brigitte; that he was agitated; that he wanted to talk to me at all costs, even if it meant here in the hospital. But the doctors wouldn't let anyone see me except Brigitte or Philipp, and that was fine by me.

Then came the time for me to start walking again. I made my way up and down the corridor, out into the garden, and around the pond, but I was worried that a rash movement might loosen whatever was clogging my arteries and send it wandering to an even more dangerous place. I knew this fear was foolish. But it was there. I was also afraid that the pain would return, that my heart might start beating irregularly, that it would stop beating altogether. I was afraid of dying.

Needless to say, while I lay there waiting, images and scenes from my life came to my mind. My childhood in Berlin, my career as public prosecutor, my marriage to Klara, my work as private investigator, my years with Brigitte. I also mulled over my last case, which I hadn't concluded the way I'd wanted to.

"I'm glad you didn't do anything to Welker," Brigitte said. "It rattled you, but it didn't kill you. You'll get back on your feet again."

It was only later that I fully understood what Brigitte meant. I wasn't reading the papers, nor watching or listening to the news. But one day I came across an old copy of the *Mannheimer Morgen* lying on a bench in the garden and the headline caught my eye: EXPLOSION IN SCHWETZINGEN. I read that a bomb had exploded in a bank in Schwetzingen. Nobody had been seriously injured, but there was extensive damage. The culprit, a recently fired employee, was detained on the scene with minor injuries by other employees and arrested by the police. The bomb seems to have gone off sooner than he expected. The lead article focused on the matter of the bomb: it was the wrong way to respond to a dismissal, regardless of whether the dismissal was justified or not. But the article pointed out that the culprit was from Cottbus, and that citizens from the former East Germany, after forty-five years of Communism, often found it difficult to come to terms with the open labor market and often regarded a dismissal as a stain on their honor. The article went on to make a few insightful remarks about crimes for lost honor.

I sat on the bench and thought about Karl-Heinz Ulbrich. I would ask Brigitte to go visit him in prison and take him a good book, a good Bordeaux, and some fresh fruit. I wanted her to take him a chess set, too, and my Spassky vs. Korchnoi. Chess was widely played in the East. I wanted her to ask Nägelsbach to put in a good word with his former colleagues. Crimes committed because of a loss of honor—the writer of that article didn't know how right he was.

I had to return to my room, where the lady doctor handed me a release to sign absolving them of all responsibility. I thought that was all she wanted, but then she checked my heart, took my blood pressure, and examined my behind.

The following morning one of the nurses shaved my chest, stomach, pubic hair, and thighs, which had been already shaved for the angiogram. Brigitte had to leave the room, as if this ultimate nakedness might reveal something dreadful. When I sat up and looked down at myself, I was moved by my hairless, defenseless organ. I was so moved that I was on the brink of tears. I realized that they had put a sedative in my drip.

Brigitte walked next to me as far as the elevator, and the male nurse wheeled me in at an angle from which I could still see her until the doors closed. She blew me a kiss.

In the elevator I grew sleepy. I can still remember being wheeled out of the elevator through a corridor into the operating theater and being lifted onto the operating table. The last thing I remember is the harsh light of the lamp overhead and the doctors' faces with masks and caps, with peering eyes whose expressions I couldn't figure out. Perhaps there wasn't anything to figure out. The doctors began their work.

21

In the end

In the end I did head back there.

Why? I knew all there was to know, and if I hadn't, the Schlossplatz would not have told me anything. I already knew that Welker had fired half his staff and sold the Sorbian bank. That he had dissolved Weller & Welker. That his house in the Gustav-Kirchhoff Strasse is up for sale and that he's moved away with his children—to Costa Rica, Brigitte says, and that his wife is still alive and waiting for him there.

I also knew that Ulbrich hadn't breathed a word to the police or the public prosecutor. Not a word. Brigitte had asked me: "Weren't you a public prosecutor once? Can't you defend him?" I made inquiries and found that I could get licensed as a lawyer. The fact that Welker had left town would make the defense easier.

What was I looking for on Schwetzingen's Schlossplatz? The end of this story? It had come to an end. None of the threads of fate had been left dangling. But though I knew at the end of a story justice didn't always have to win out, I could not accept as an ending that Welker would get away with what he'd done while Ulbrich was in jail and Schuler and Samarin were dead and buried. Again I was tortured by the powerlessness of not being able to do anything anymore, not being able to fix things.

Until I realized that it was my decision whether I would interpret the ending as unjust and unsatisfactory and suffer because of it or decided that this, and only this, was the fitting ending. In either case it was my decision. Even Welker dead or Welker in prison, and a happy Karl-Heinz Ulbrich, and a Schuler who went on cultivating his files, and a Samarin who went on laundering money were not entirely just and satisfactory. I was the one who would have to decide. So I tried. I didn't accept the end without question. But wasn't there something fitting about Samarin, a warrior, being killed in action, and Schuler having died for the truth that lay hidden in his beloved archive? It could be arranged that Ulbrich wouldn't have to stay in prison for too long. As for Welker? Brigitte and I could go to Costa Rica on vacation.

If the doctor allows it. He's an old friend of Philipp's and was a colleague of his in Mannheim before Philipp took over the department at the Speyerer Hof Clinic. The doctor shakes his head and shrugs his shoulders when I ask him about my condition and what I am to expect.

"What can I say, Herr Self? Your heart is worn out."

Worn out. I'm quite aware that the operation wasn't a success. Otherwise they would have told me. And I wouldn't have been so tired. Sometimes I feel as if my tiredness is out to poison me.

I was happy when the taxi arrived.